CLEAR SKIES

CLEAR SKIES

Jessica Scott Kerrin

Groundwood Books
House of Anansi Press
Toronto   Berkeley

Groundwood Books / House of Anansi Press
groundwoodbooks.com

We gratefully acknowledge for their financial support of our publishing
program the Canada Council for the Arts, the Ontario Arts Council and the
Government of Canada.

Library and Archives Canada Cataloguing in Publication
Title: Clear skies / Jessica Scott Kerrin.
Names: Kerrin, Jessica Scott, author.
Identifiers: Canadiana (print) 20189067357 | Canadiana (ebook)
20189067365 | ISBN 9781773062402 (hardcover) | ISBN 9781773062419
(EPUB) | ISBN 9781773062426 (Kindle)
Classification: LCC PS8621.E77 C54 2019 | DDC jC813/.6—dc23

Design by Michael Solomon
Interior illustrations by Emma Sakamoto
Jacket illustration by Katy Dockrill

Groundwood Books is committed to protecting our natural environment.
As part of our efforts, the interior of this book is printed on paper that
contains 100% post-consumer recycled fibers, is acid-free and is processed
chlorine-free.

Printed and bound in Canada

In memory of Sheila Barry,
now among the stars

ONE

ARNO CREELMAN'S DEEP THOUGHTS

Gravity is a force that pulls objects like stars and planets together. The bigger the mass, the stronger the pull. So why is our universe expanding, with galaxies moving away from each other?

What goes up must come down.

ARNO SLAPPED A pound of wet clay into the shape of a ball, then plopped the ball onto his desk with a satisfying *whump*. He peered at the open astronomy book beside his lump of clay to read the instructions once again.

Divide the clay into ten equal parts.

"Okay-dokey," Arno whispered.

He was being quiet so that he could hear his dad's yellow-and-red Sony transistor radio.

It was 1961. The Space Race between the Soviet Union and the United States was in full swing. Over the past few years, artificial satellites had been launched. The *Saturn I* rocket, meant to carry human beings into deep space, was well under construction. Soviet pilots had even flown into low Earth orbit as test trials.

Which country would be the first to safely land someone on the Moon and bring them back was anybody's guess.

And in all this excitement, a brand-new observatory was opening the following night in Arno's

11

hometown. It had been built in a wide field on the outskirts where there was no light pollution to interfere with the powerful telescope housed in its dome.

Arno desperately wanted to go to the opening, not only because he planned to become an astronomer when he grew up, but also because his hero, Jean Slayter-Appleton, was flying in as the honored guest to cut the ribbon.

Jean Slayter-Appleton wrote a weekly column about astronomy in the newspaper. Her column was called "Clear Skies." She ended every article with those two words.

Clear skies were what every astronomer wished for when they set up their telescopes to point at the stars.

Arno clipped all of her articles for his notebook, which contained his deep thoughts about how the universe worked. He would quote fascinating facts from her column whenever he got the chance.

Arno paused to listen to the radio. The station was giving away three invitations to attend the opening of the observatory for contest winners and their guests. All he had to do was be the first to call in with the correct answer to an astronomy-related question that the announcer would ask some time throughout the morning.

For now, only surf rock music about girls and cars blared from the transistor radio. Arno turned back to his lump of clay and divided it up like the instructions told him to do. He read from his book again.

Mash six of the parts together and put that on Jupiter's sheet of paper.

Arno had already spread out nine sheets of paper on his desk. He had written the name of a planet on each one.

He mashed the six lumps together as instructed and set it on Jupiter's paper. He paused to listen to the radio.

More surf rock.

Mash three of the parts together and put that on Saturn's sheet.

Arno did so.

Divide the remaining piece into ten equal parts.

Arno did that, too, just as his frisky dog pitter-pattered into Arno's bedroom.

Comet immediately sniffed the wet clay on Arno's desk and wagged his tail like an exclamation mark.

"Leave it," Arno warned, pushing Comet's nose away.

Comet was little and he couldn't reach the top of Arno's desk, but still. Arno had once caught him sliding a kitchen chair toward the counter so that he could jump on it to reach some fresh-baked cookies cooling on the racks.

Comet perked his triangle-folded ears but backed down. Muttering, he trotted over to the foot of Arno's bed and flopped to the floor, his head resting on both front paws while he watched Arno's every move.

Arno paused. The radio music had stopped.

The announcer was delivering news and the weather, which called for another unbearably hot August day.

Arno held his breath. Was the contest about to begin?

No. After the weather came sports and then more surf rock music.

"Blast it!" Arno exclaimed.

Comet lifted his head, saw that nothing was happening, then rolled onto his side and closed his eyes for a nap.

Arno returned to his book, which helped keep his jitters in check.

Add five parts to Saturn's lump. Mash two parts together and put them on Neptune's sheet. Mash two more parts together and put them on the sheet for Uranus. Take the remaining piece and divide it into ten equal parts.

Arno carefully followed the instructions. Four of the nine planets in the solar system were starting to take shape on their respective pieces of paper.

"Okay, Arno. I'm heading out now."

Arno looked up. His dad was standing at the door in his blue-and-white delivery uniform. Comet scrambled to his paws, then dashed across the floor to greet him, his tail wagging furiously.

"I've already fed Comet his breakfast," his dad said, bending to give the dog a pat. "So don't let him fool you."

"Uh-huh," Arno said, turning back to his project.

"Remember to make your bed. And promise me you'll get outside," his dad added. "Today is going to be too beautiful to waste."

"I won't waste it. I'm building an accurate model of the solar system." Arno held up a wet lump of clay.

"Right," his dad said, checking his watch. He went over to ruffle the top of Arno's head. "I'll be home for lunch."

Arno was half listening, what with the demands of building planets and monitoring the radio at the same time. He only vaguely heard the sound of his dad's van pulling out of the driveway. It had big logos on both sides.

Stinky's.

Arno's dad ran a diaper-cleaning service. People left bins of soiled cloth diapers and empty baskets on their front steps for pickup. His small fleet of vans cruised the suburbs, replacing them with empty bins and baskets full of soft, freshly laundered diapers.

Arno used to like riding shotgun, but today he sighed in relief as the van drove off without him. He remembered the last time he helped with deliveries.

Arno had been rearranging the towering stacks of baskets in the back of the van while his dad rang the doorbell of a new customer. A sudden wind pushed the van's back door shut with a surprising bang, trapping Arno inside the airless, windowless space.

Arno froze. Everything was black. At first he only heard the sound of his breath. Then his heart started to pound in his ears. He clutched at his chest, which began to feel tight, as if something was pressing down on him. He couldn't catch his breath. He imagined the baskets toppling on top of him if he so much as budged.

And what if they did? He'd be crushed! That thought was so frightening, he couldn't even call out for help. Instead he frantically banged on the walls of the van until his startled dad rushed to his rescue.

That wasn't the only time Arno had panicked. His first attack happened back in the spring when one of his older twin brothers, home from college, wrestled Arno to the ground after he discovered that Arno had drunk the last of the milk, leaving his brother nothing for his cereal.

"Serves you right for sleeping in," Arno taunted.

His brother tried to give Arno a wedgie, but Arno squirmed so furiously that he resorted to pinning Arno down with a heavy wool blanket over his head. It was a new move.

Arno would have preferred the wedgie. The thick blanket pressed against his face as if already soaked in his sweat, entombing his every breath and trapping his one and only thought. He was surely going to die if he didn't escape quickly.

His brother sat on Arno in victory and whooped.

"Get off!" Arno tried to yell, but the words stuck in his throat.

"Say uncle!"

But Arno couldn't. Instead, he burst into hysterics. It even frightened his brother, who rolled off and apologized.

Arno hoped his fright was a one-time thing, but after his second panic attack in the van, he looked up his symptoms at the library.

Claustrophobia.

A fear of tight spaces.

So? Everyone was afraid of something, Arno figured. His mom was scared of birds in the house, so she badgered him about keeping the screen door shut. His dad was scared of horror movies, so he would only take them to drive-ins that showed musicals or comedies.

Both of them coped by avoiding the things that frightened them. It seemed to work.

And that's what Arno would do, too.

Just avoid tight spaces.

No big deal.

Arno listened a beat, his hands wet with clay, as his dad put the van into first gear and drove away.

Freedom! Arno smiled.

Arno's mom was away, helping his Aunt Faye with her new baby in Ferndale. It meant that

Arno had the whole house to himself, at least until lunch. He had no intention of going outside in the scorching heat. Not until his solar system was done, at any rate. And making his bed was at the rock bottom of his list.

Arno returned to his book.

Take nine parts and add them to Saturn's lump. Divide the remaining piece into two equal parts.

Arno did so, all the while listening for the radio announcer to come back on. Comet, who had followed Arno's dad to the door, returned to Arno's room and eyeballed Saturn.

"Don't even think about it," Arno warned without glancing up from his book.

Comet reluctantly sat, as if he was on the lookout for the right moment.

Comet was sly.

And patient.

Put one piece on Earth's sheet. Divide the remaining piece into ten.

Arno paused to admire the completed globes. Earth was so tiny compared to Jupiter! He hugged the book to his chest in a moment of pure happiness. Each chapter promised a hands-on activity guaranteed to help unlock the universe. And he had the rest of the summer!

Arno set the book back down and continued to read.

Mash nine pieces together and place on Venus's sheet. Divide the remaining piece into ten equal parts.

The endless music continued to play, as if the radio announcer had gone on a long coffee break.

Mash nine parts together to make Mars.

Arno admired his work some more. Meanwhile, the music ended and the announcer returned to the mike.

This was it! Arno stood, ready for the question.

"Our sun is like the vast majority of stars, a gigantic ball of hydrogen and helium elements all held together by gravity and creating light and heat in a process called nuclear fusion. But, dear listener, how old, exactly, is our sun?"

"It's 4.5 billion years old!" Arno shouted.

Jean Slayter-Appleton had written about it in one of her columns. She had also written that the Sun accounted for ninety-nine percent of all the matter in the solar system, and that the rest of the planets, moons, asteroids and comets added together made up the remaining one percent. That was why they revolved around the Sun. It had the most mass and therefore the strongest gravitational pull.

But that was beside the point.

Arno dashed into the kitchen and was about the grab the telephone mounted on the wall to call in his answer when he realized that his hands were covered in wet clay. He ran to the sink to wash them. By the time he called the radio station's number, all he got was the busy signal.

Too late.

"Blast it!" Arno shouted in the empty kitchen.

He returned to his room, his incomplete solar system somehow looking less exciting now. The radio announcer was congratulating the winner. He went on to say that the Sun was 109 times wider than Earth and that it was middle-aged.

"I knew that, too," Arno muttered. "The Sun's going to burn out in five billion years, give or take." Arno turned to Comet, who always listened with fascination to anything Arno said about the universe. "And when it does, it's going to swell until it engulfs the orbits of Mercury, Venus and Earth to eventually become a white dwarf star."

Comet applauded with several tail wags.

The radio returned to playing music.

"Blast it," Arno said again, shoulders slumping.

Comet trotted over to lick his hand.

"It's okay, Comet," Arno said, scratching behind the dog's ears. "It's not over yet. There'll be two more chances. We just need to be vigilant."

Comet shook his ears. Vigilant was his middle name.

Arno picked up the remaining piece of clay, which was very small indeed. He read from his book.

Divide the last piece into ten equal parts. Mash nine of those pieces to make Mercury. Place the only piece left on Pluto's sheet.

"Wow," Arno said. "Look at you, teeny tiny Pluto. You're barely a planet at all!"

But wait. Where was Saturn?

Arno wheeled around to survey his room.

"Comet!" he shouted, just as his dog, Saturn in his mouth, dashed under Arno's bed. "Give it back, Comet!"

He knelt down to peer at Comet. Comet scooted farther back into the darkness. He gently held Saturn by the tips of his pointy little teeth.

"I mean it, Comet. Bad dog! Give it back!"

Arno thrust his arm under the bed like he meant business, but his sweeping hand came nowhere near Comet.

"Don't make me come after you!"

Comet thumped his tail in glee but otherwise didn't budge.

The solar system was nothing without Saturn. Arno peered under the bed to survey the situation.

It was dark under there. It was a small space. He might get stuck with no one home to rescue him.

And then what?

His heart started to race, just like it had at the thought of tumbling baskets back in the van. He remembered the feeling of the heavy wool blanket over his head. His neck became clammy and his mouth went dry.

Parched, even.

The doorbell rang.

Comet dropped Saturn like yesterday's newspaper, then scooted out from under the bed to race to the front door.

Arno studied Saturn's location. It was still way out of his reach, and the bed was too heavy to move.

He stood.

"I'll get it later," Arno muttered.

He went to answer the door.

TWO

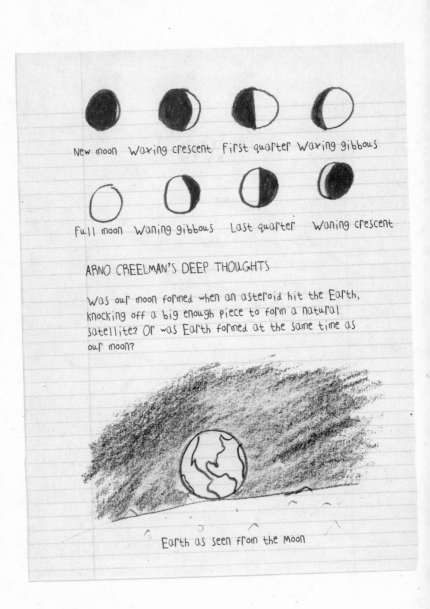

New moon   Waxing crescent   First quarter   Waxing gibbous

Full moon   Waning gibbous   Last quarter   Waning crescent

ARNO CREELMAN'S DEEP THOUGHTS

Was our moon formed when an asteroid hit the Earth, knocking off a big enough piece to form a natural satellite? Or was Earth formed at the same time as our moon?

Earth as seen from the Moon

BUDDY CLARK STOOD at the door with beads of sweat on his forehead and a peeling nose from a nasty sunburn. He was wearing shorts and his ridiculous cowboy boots. They made his knobby legs look even skinnier.

"Hey, Arno."

"Hey, Buddy."

"Hey, Comet."

Comet jumped up on Buddy, who held out his hands for Comet to lick, which Comet vigorously did.

Buddy took Comet's enthusiasm as an invitation to come in. He rough-housed with Comet for a bit, then galumphed down the hall, not bothering to take off his dopey boots.

Comet scampered after him, his claws making *clippity-clip* sounds on the polished linoleum floor.

"It's going to be another scorcher," Buddy said over his shoulder as he beelined it to Arno's kitchen. "Is your mom still away?" He yanked the fridge door open and peered inside.

27

The fridge was chock-a-block full of tinfoil-covered meals that Arno's mom had prepared before she left.

"Yeah," Arno said, trailing him into the kitchen after retrieving the transistor radio from his room. He set the radio on the kitchen counter. "Careful you don't scuff the floors."

Buddy still needed reminders like that. It drove Arno nuts. If Buddy wasn't the only other boy on the block who was Arno's age, Arno probably wouldn't have to spend so much time with him.

But summers were long and friends were in short supply, so there they were.

"Got any Tang?" Buddy asked.

Buddy brought up Tang whenever he could. His dad worked for an advertising agency that got celebrities to say they used various products to boost sales. NASA planned to send up different foods with astronauts to see how eating was affected in low gravity. His dad was trying to convince NASA that astronauts should include Tang in those experiments.

"No Tang," Arno said, but he was thirsty, too. "I'll make lemonade."

"Lemonade?" Buddy scoffed. "Get with the times, Arno. It's the Space Age. Once NASA signs up with Tang, it's going to be everyone's favorite instant breakfast drink. It has real orange flavor."

Unlike Arno, Buddy wanted to be an astronaut when he grew up. When he found out that NASA's new Manned Spacecraft Center — the home of Mission Control Center for the US human spaceflight program — was located in Texas, he begged for a pair of cowboy boots for his eleventh birthday. They lived nowhere near Texas, but he had been parading around in his stupid boots ever since.

Arno didn't think Buddy would make the grade. After all, astronauts were the *crème de la crème* of fighter pilots. They were top dogs. Only test pilots could apply for the Project Mercury mission, and just seven of the five hundred who did were selected. From what Arno could tell, they didn't clomp around in ridiculous cowboy boots that rubbed their bare calves red.

Arno plucked his mom's handwritten recipe card for lemonade from the fridge door where she had taped it next to Aunt Faye's phone number written in gigantic orange crayon.

"I'm making lemonade. Want some or not?"

Buddy sighed, as if this was the worst news since the Soviets successfully launched the first astronaut into outer space months ago, ahead of the Americans.

"So you don't have any Tang?"

"Correct."

Buddy sighed again.

"Just lemonade?"

"Roger that."

Buddy rocked on his heels, contemplating his choices.

"Aren't your feet sweaty?" Arno asked.

"Nope," Buddy said, looking down to admire his gaudy boots. Then he smiled, which reminded Arno of a toad. Toads always smiled no matter what they were thinking.

Arno pulled the lemons from the fruit bowl and read the recipe out loud to ward off further conversation about astronauts, which he knew was the only thing that Buddy liked to talk about.

10 lemons.

1 cup superfine sugar.

2 cups cold water.

Ice.

Strain the lemon juice through a fine sieve into a pitcher to get rid of the pulp and seeds.

Add sugar, stirring until it dissolves.

Stir in the water, then the ice.

Top with sprigs of fresh mint from the garden.

"I guess I'll have some," Buddy said grudgingly, sitting down at the kitchen table. "If that's all you're making."

Arno said nothing. He had learned to let Buddy's comments bounce off him like meteoroids ricocheting off Earth's outer atmosphere.

He grabbed the first lemon. When he sliced it cleanly in two, the lemon exhaled its tart warning into the dry summer air. He placed one half on the reamer of his juice press. He took a deep, steadying breath and cautiously cranked the press.

"Blast it!" Arno hollered, blinking furiously after he was squirted right in the eye.

He blindly grasped for the faucet and turned on the water to splash his face. Nothing burned like the sting from an angry ripe lemon.

Comet, who had settled on his bed in the corner, drooped his ears and whimpered in sympathy.

"Guess what doesn't sting when you make it?" Buddy said as he leaned back in his chair, his cowboy boots making scuff marks beneath the table.

Arno ignored him.

When the stinging subsided, Arno turned off the faucet and reached for a tea towel to pat himself dry. The towel smelled of laundry soap and sunshine.

31

Undaunted, he placed the other half onto the reamer to wring out the juice. He turned the crank so slowly, it was like watching the Moon rise in the night sky.

At first the lemon squeezed perfectly. A miracle!

But then Arno got cocky. He cranked a little faster and took another squirt to the eye.

The *other* eye.

"Blast it!" he bellowed, rubbing furiously, blinking back tears.

Comet sadly tilted his head, his golden eyes softly trained on Arno.

"With Tang, all you do is pour the crystals into ice-cold water, stir, and presto. You're done," Buddy declared. He picked at a scab forming at the back of his leg where the top of his cowboy boot rubbed and flicked it onto the floor near the scuff marks.

Arno ran more water at the kitchen sink to splash his face.

"Enough with the Tang," Arno growled. "One more word and you'll get nothing."

Buddy didn't flinch. He seemed to like pushing Arno's buttons.

After the lemonade was made with several more squirts to the eyes, Arno poured two tall glasses. The boys carried them and the pitcher out to the shaded front porch where it was a few degrees cooler. They sat in the two wooden chairs that were planted side by side. A small table stacked with magazines was wedged between them. Comet stretched out under Arno's legs.

Even though it was still morning, the Sun blazed. Grasshoppers buzzed loudly in waves.

There was no breeze, not even a puff.

The street was empty. Everyone was staying inside, hiding from the punishing heat.

"Bet I can hold off taking a sip before you do," Buddy said, turning to Arno. Buddy was always up for a competition that required some kind of physical endurance. He'd go on and on about how astronauts faced hardships all the time.

Arno gave Buddy a level glare, then took a long, delicious sip. He smacked his lips and said, "Ahhhhh." He took another long sip.

Besides, he knew that Buddy would win any physical competition hands down. Buddy had proved this to everyone when he entered the school's Spring Fling fundraiser several months ago.

A local bicycle shop had donated a Raleigh Deluxe Space Rider to the school. The three-speed came with white sidewall roadster tires, a multi-spring saddle, a kit bag for tools and a pump, a lamp bracket with a generator light and a kickstand.

"It's even painted a metallic color called Neptune Blue," Arno told his parents over dinner after he saw it on display.

Everyone agreed it was the bike to have.

The school then sold tickets for an endurance contest in which the bike stood in the gymnasium, and participants had to continuously touch a part of the bike for as long as possible. If a participant let go of the bike even for a split second, that contestant was out of the competition.

The rules were clear. Contestants were only allowed ten-minute washroom breaks once every hour. The person who held on the longest would win the bike.

At the start of the competition, there must have been thirty kids jammed together and jockeying for space while touching a part of the coveted bike. The rest of the school sat on bleachers in the gym and cheered them on. The school band played to keep everyone entertained, and the parents' association sold popcorn.

About half of the contestants quit within the first fifteen minutes, including Arno. The crowd of kids pressing in made his stomach start to twist. As much as he wanted that bike, he did not want to risk being embarrassed by having a panic attack in front of the entire school.

Another quarter of the contestants quit within an hour. More trickled away as time passed.

Then it was down to six kids.

Mindy Venetia.

Anton Spagnolli.

Heimlich Fester.

Sam Preeble.

Abe Wooster.

And Buddy Clark.

All six grabbed hold as if they were astronauts in a space capsule seizing the controls during the final countdown. Except this went on for hours, well into the afternoon. The crowd began to thin and the popcorn ran out. It was getting close to dinnertime.

Something had to be done.

"New rules," the principal announced into the microphone. "Contestants must now keep *both* hands on the bike."

The thinning crowd murmured their approval.

All six contestants clamped both hands on the prize, determined as ever.

Minutes later, Mindy sneezed. She politely covered her mouth with her hand.

"Bless you," Buddy said, and he chuckled.

Mindy was out.

"No fair!" she complained.

The loud round of applause put a quick end to her protests.

Anton Spagnolli got a charley horse from sitting cross-legged so long. He, too, was out when he rubbed his calf for relief.

"What a shame," Buddy said, then grinned from ear to ear.

The audience applauded. Anton was out.

Heimlich Fester fell asleep and rolled over.

"Sweet dreams," Buddy teased, poking Heimlich with his foot.

More applause. Heimlich was out.

Then Sam Preeble and Abe Wooster failed to return with Buddy after their ten-minute washroom break. The audience assumed the two had quit.

Buddy won the bike.

Only later did everyone learn that Sam and Abe had somehow been locked inside the boys' washroom. The janitor came to their rescue after he happened to find his mislaid keys by the water fountain near the washroom and heard them pounding on the door.

Arno still couldn't shake his suspicions about who had locked those two boys inside.

That Raleigh Deluxe Space Rider was now leaning against Arno's front porch. Buddy never went anywhere without it, constantly popping wheelies for anyone who was willing to watch.

"Astronauts have phenomenal lung capacity," Buddy said after taking his own sip of lemonade. "You know how —"

"Your dad once met John Glenn," Arno answered quickly, because he knew Buddy was dying to tell him all about it.

Again.

Arno did not relish hearing in great detail about the time Buddy's dad sat in on a meeting with NASA officials at the Manned Spacecraft Center about the Tang account, and later spotted John Glenn in the elevator.

Given the chance, Buddy would report that John Glenn had even *spoken* to Buddy's dad after Buddy's dad introduced himself. The astronaut replied, "Nice to meet you," and shook his dad's hand.

"It was out of this world!" Buddy would say.

Arno leaned over to turn up his radio.

"I have great lung capacity, too," Buddy said, unphased by the blaring music. He yelled above it. "Want to see me perform the astronaut balloon test?"

He didn't wait for an answer. He dug out several rubber balloons from his pocket. They were orange with Tang's brand printed on each one. He began to blow them up, one by one. His face got redder and redder.

"Look," Buddy said between balloons, his chest heaving. "I'm not even winded."

He was blowing up the fifth balloon when Arno realized that the music on the radio had ended, and that the announcer was asking another astronomy question.

"Shhhhh!" Arno insisted, reaching over with both hands to pop the balloon from Buddy's mouth.

The balloon zoomed off the porch and landed beside the Raleigh Deluxe Space Rider.

"You can think of the Moon as Earth's only natural satellite," the announcer said. "It is relatively big, being the fifth-largest satellite in our solar system. But, dear listener, why can we see only one side?"

"Because the other side is dark!" Buddy exclaimed.

"Wrong!" Arno shouted as he rushed into the kitchen to call the radio station. "It's because the time the Moon takes to rotate on its axis is around the same length of time it takes to orbit Earth!"

His hands were shaking as he dialed.

Busy signal.

Too late.

"Blast it!" he shouted. If he hadn't been distracted by Buddy, he might have reached the telephone sooner.

"So, there isn't really a dark side?" Buddy asked, following Arno into the kitchen.

"No," Arno grumbled, both hands planted on the counter, his head hanging. "It's just the far side we can't see from here."

"Oh, good," Buddy said. "When I become an astronaut, that's the side I'm going to visit."

Buddy smiled like a toad as he rocked back on his scuff marks.

THREE

ARNO CREELMAN'S DEEP THOUGHTS

Just because we don't have a scientific explanation right now, it doesn't mean there isn't one to discover.

Why is our universe so big? Most stars have a twin. Why does the Earth only have one sun?

Sun will explode in 5 billion years, engulfing Earth

THE DAY WAS getting hotter by the minute. Even on Arno's shady front porch, the heat was strong enough to blast both boys back in their chairs, as if they'd been hit by a solar flare.

A trickle of sweat ran down between Arno's shoulder blades. Comet lay sprawled beneath his legs, flattening himself against the wood deck, his pink tongue lolling out. A fierce sunbeam inched steadily toward the little dog's water bowl while neighborhood cats sought shade beneath parked cars on the street.

Arno concentrated on listening to the radio, which was now playing one Motown band after another. Buddy reached for the top copy from Arno's well-worn collection of *Life* magazines stacked on the table between them. Arno saved all the copies that featured something about outer space on the cover.

Buddy flipped to an article about the Mercury Seven. He read how the American astronauts were being tested in a heat chamber as part of getting ready to fly into outer space. He studied the photos of men who had been zipped into spacesuits and were being strapped inside the chamber.

"What a tight squeeze," Buddy said, holding out the magazine to Arno for a look. "My dad told me that astronauts have to be 5 feet 11 inches or shorter so that they can fit into the spacecraft. Lucky for me, my dad is only 5 feet 9."

"Yeah. I don't think you have anything to worry about," Arno said.

Buddy was, by far, the shortest boy in their class.

Although the astronauts were smiling and giving the photographer the A-OK sign, it only took one look for Arno to feel the beginnings of panic flutter in his stomach. He would be terrified, strapped into a chair that was bolted to the floor, then locked inside that cramped chamber. The mere thought made him want to throw up. It was a powerful reminder about why becoming an astronomer was so much better. Arno would still be able to see everything in the universe, only he would do so from wide-open fields on Earth.

Arno pushed the magazine back toward Buddy.

"Read on your own," he said gruffly. He closed his eyes to better concentrate on the radio.

Buddy settled into his chair and flipped to an article Arno had already read about Yuri Gagarin, a Soviet cosmonaut who had been launched in a rocket ship that spring and made over seventeen orbits around Earth before ejecting himself and parachuting to the ground separately from his capsule. Then Buddy read out loud the part about American navy commander Alan B. Shepard Jr., who followed the Soviets by rocketing away from Earth's surface a few weeks later on top of a Mercury-Redstone rocket. Shepard's fifteen-minute spaceflight reached a high altitude, yet his spacecraft, *Freedom 7*, wasn't fast enough to achieve orbit.

Buddy was about to continue, but he was interrupted by the sounds of a heavy diesel engine. A moving van came rumbling down their street. It backed into a driveway five houses from where Arno lived — a house that looked much like his but with a Sold sign planted in its browned-out front lawn.

Arno put down his glass of lemonade, and Buddy closed his magazine to watch.

The movers unloaded a kitchen table set with tubular steel legs and molded plastic seats, a starburst wall clock, baked enamel cabinets with

45

sliding plate-glass doors, pole lamps with fern-green shades, plaid swivel chairs, matching avocado-colored appliances and a long sleek couch in gold fabric.

Then a glossy white station wagon with skylight windows pulled up in front of the house. When a family of four tumbled out — a dad, a mom, a boy and his older sister who was wearing a tall beehive held back with a hairband, Arno could see that the interior of the car was racy red.

"Do be careful, lads!" the dad warned, dogging the movers as they carried a television in through the propped-open front door.

Arno wasn't all that impressed. Almost every house on his street owned a television by now. What was more unusual was that the dad had an accent that sounded like the Queen of England.

As soon as a bicycle was unloaded from the moving van, the boy grabbed it and climbed on. He pedaled lazy figure-eights in the empty street, heat waves wafting up from the softening black pavement, until he spotted Arno and Buddy. He charged straight toward them.

"Hello!" he called out, coming to a full stop on the sidewalk in front of Arno's house.

"Hi," Arno said, tugging at his sweaty T-shirt.

Comet lifted his head but was too hot to move from beneath Arno's legs. Buddy just stared with his mouth open.

Arno knew that they should be a titch more friendly.

"Welcome to the neighborhood," he added.

"Thanks." The boy got off his bike and pulled out the kickstand. He walked up to the porch, stood on the top step and thrust out his hand. "I'm Robert Fines. That's my house," he said, nodding in the direction of the movers.

Robert had an accent, too, but not as strong as his dad's. "House" sounded like "howse," not "hoos," which was how Arno and his friends said it.

"I'm Arno Creelman," Arno said, reluctantly standing up to shake hands because his own was so sweaty.

"Buddy Clark," Buddy said, doing the same after wiping his brow with a corner of his shirt.

Robert ran his fingers through a huge cowlick. His ears stuck out, glowing pink in the sun, and when he smiled, Arno saw there was a small gap between his two front teeth.

"Is that your dog?" Robert asked, crouching down to peer at Comet. He said "dahg," not "dowg."

47

Comet gave two thumps of his tail but otherwise stayed put.

"Yeah," Arno said.

"What's his name?" Robert pressed.

"Comet."

"Sorry. Did you say Comet?"

"Yeah. He was born the year two really bright comets were spotted in 1957. They came close and could even be seen by the naked eye. And they were the first ones since Halley's Comet back in 1910."

"Here we go," Buddy muttered.

"What?" Arno asked, wheeling around to catch Buddy rolling his eyes.

"Hey, Robert," Buddy said, settling back into his chair. "Check this out." He held his hands palms up and tilted his head. "Say, Arno? What are comets?"

Arno took the bait.

"Fun fact. The word *comet* is very old. It comes from the Greek word meaning hairy, a hairy star. Comets are leftovers from the formation of our solar system 4.6 billion years ago. They move around the Sun and are made up of ice mixed with dust. As they move past Jupiter, they begin to defrost, and when they approach the orbit of

Mars, they start to form long tails. Blown by the solar wind from our sun, the tails of comets always point away from the heat. Halley's Comet is famous because it returns within a human lifetime. Do you know when it will next come back?"

"Beats me," Buddy said. He winked at Robert, who stood with his eyes wide open, eyebrows raised.

"Halley's Comet appears to Earth about every seventy-five years. Right now it's too faint to be seen, but it will return in 1986."

With that, Arno sat down.

"And by then I'll have left my footprints on the Moon." Buddy smiled his toad smile. "Careful what you ask about around here, Robert," he added, nodding toward Arno. "You'll get way more than you bargained for."

"I'll keep that in mind," Robert said. "Are you *both* outer space fans?"

Arno nodded, and Buddy added, "My dad met John Glenn. I'm going to be an astronaut just like him."

"You, too?" Robert asked, turning to Arno.

"No," Arno said. "An astronomer."

"Astronomer. Astronaut. Cool. But it's astrology that's boss."

Arno and Buddy leaned forward, wrinkled their brows and together said, "What?"

"Astrology. The study of the movements and positions of planets that impact us and our natural world."

"Do you mean like how the Moon pulls on the oceans to make tides?" Arno asked.

"It's far more than that!"

Both boys looked at him blankly.

"Our entire personality depends on the planets' locations when we're born."

This took some time to sink in, and then Buddy started to laugh.

"You can't be serious!"

"Check it out. What's your zodiac sign?"

Buddy stopped laughing.

"My what?"

"When's your birthday?"

"April Fool's Day," Buddy boasted.

Arno could never understand why Buddy didn't see how that was so funny.

"So, April 1st. That makes you an Aries," Robert said. "Aries are eager, quick, dynamic and competitive. Does that describe you?"

Buddy widened his eyes. "You're right!" he said.

"And when's your birthday?" Robert asked Arno.

"September 18th."

"That makes you a Virgo. Virgos are practical, loyal, gentle and analytical."

Arno said nothing.

I'm all those things, he thought.

Still, Robert must have used some kind of trick. But how?

"Nifty, huh?" Robert said smugly. Then he added, "Phew. I'm roasting." He eyeballed Arno's pitcher of lemonade sweating on the table next to the magazines.

"Do you want some?" Arno asked, still trying to figure out how on earth Robert had got those things right. It sure wasn't because of phony-baloney astrology, that's for sure.

"Yes, please."

"Where're you from?" Arno asked, filling a glass for Robert after retrieving one from the kitchen.

"London," Robert said.

"So, England," Arno said. He was pretty good at geography.

"No, Canada. There's a London there, too. My dad's from England. But then my parents moved to Canada. And now we're here."

Robert took a sip of lemonade. "Mmmmmm," he said.

51

"It's my mom's recipe," Arno said proudly.

"It's very ... lemony," Robert said carefully. He puckered his lips.

Was that meant to be a compliment? Arno wasn't sure.

"Yeah. That's because there are lemons in it," Arno said, more defensively than he would have liked. "Fresh lemons."

"I told you Tang was better," Buddy leaned over and whispered loudly into Arno's ear.

Arno batted him away. Smiling, Buddy poured himself another tall glass of lemonade, emptying the pitcher.

"It's primo," Robert said peering into his glass. "Really. Only, I wondered if you might want to tone down the tartness of the lemons with a bit of ginger."

"Ginger?"

"Ginger or cucumbers. Or vanilla. Have you ever tried any of those? Delicious."

Arno just stared at him, dumbfounded and annoyed.

"Just a friendly suggestion," Robert said cheerfully, setting down the glass on the porch railing. It was still mostly full. "Well, I'd better burn rubber. Sorry. Lots of unpacking to do.

Nice to meet you both."

He climbed on his bike and pedaled home.

Arno poured the rest of Robert's rejected lemonade onto the lilac bush by the steps.

Ginger? Cucumbers? Vanilla??

He looked up at his new neighbor's house, Robert's bike now abandoned on their front lawn next to the Sold sign.

"What a flake," Arno said, sitting back down.

"Polite, though," Buddy said. "Can I borrow a bucket?" he asked.

His innocent tone put Arno on high alert.

"What for?"

"Another astronaut test. They can keep their feet in ice water."

"Ice water?"

"That's an actual test. An endurance test that astronauts have to pass. Just like the balloons. So do you have a bucket or not?"

"Under the kitchen sink," Arno said, reaching for a *Life* magazine from the stack.

Buddy dashed inside. When he came back out, he was lugging a bucket filled with water and ice. He set it down on the deck, sloshing contents that splashed Comet, it was so heavy.

Comet grunted as he shifted to a drier spot.

"Want to give this a try?" Buddy asked.

"I do not," Arno said.

"Chicken."

"I'm not chicken," Arno said. "You heard Robert. I'm a Virgo. And Virgos are practical. I don't want to lose precious time drying my feet before I can run inside to the phone when they ask the last astronomy question on the radio."

"Point taken," Buddy said. "The least you can do is time me."

"No problem," Arno said, closing his magazine. He was genuinely curious about how long Buddy would torture himself. "Ready when you are."

"Hang on a sec," Buddy said.

He yanked off his idiotic boots, then repositioned the bucket of ice water. Taking a deep breath, he plunged one foot in right after the other. He made two clenched-white fists and began to screech immediately.

It was ear-splitting.

It didn't sound human.

Arno doubled over with laughter.

Buddy only stopped when he stumbled out of the bucket, water slopping across the deck. Comet perked up to scavenge a few spilled ice cubes that skittered his way.

"How many seconds?" Buddy asked after sitting down to rub his feet.

"I forgot to count," Arno admitted after he finally stopped laughing. "You sounded like Comet if he breathed in helium from a balloon and started barking at a cat."

"Buddy! Lunch!" Buddy's mother hollered from the front porch of Buddy's house, which was up the block in the opposite direction from Robert's.

"Thanks for nothing," Buddy said, picking up his boots. He made his way barefoot down the steps and onto the boiling sidewalk. "Hot, hot, hot!" he yelped before he could jump on his bike and pedal home.

Arno sat back in his chair just as the music on his transistor radio, along with his last chance to win the contest, died.

There was nothing but silence, followed by the buzz of grasshoppers.

"Blast it!" Arno yelled, jumping up, the sweaty backs of his legs peeling off the seat. "My batteries!"

FOUR

ARNO CREELMAN'S DEEP THOUGHTS

Is there intelligent life on another planet in another solar system? Would that world be more advanced? Are they watching us now? Or are we too close to the Sun for them to ever spot?

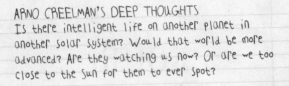

ARNO WAS ROOTING through every drawer in the kitchen in a frantic search for batteries when his dad arrived home for lunch. By then, Arno had emptied most of the contents onto the kitchen counters and pawed through everything, leaving a jumbled mess.

"Whoa! What's going on?" Arno's dad asked while Comet leapt all around his legs.

"My batteries died!" Arno cried. He held up the dead transistor radio.

"Why the panic?"

"There's a contest for tickets to tomorrow night's opening of the new observatory! They could ask an astronomy question any minute! I have to be the first to phone in, and I already missed out on the first two questions! This is my last chance!!"

"I see." Arno's dad took the radio and popped off the back cover. "This needs a 9-volt. And I don't know where your mother keeps the spares."

He went to the sink to wash his hands.

"But I need one!" Arno said, close to crumbling.

"What about your toys? Some of them take batteries, don't they? Maybe your Show Me projector?"

Arno had been given a toy projector two birthdays ago. It was battery-operated and came with short strips of cartoon cells with information written on them, set in cardboard so they could slide in and out of the projector. One of the sets that Arno bought later was a month-by-month depiction of all eighty-eight constellations.

"No. That takes three D batteries. But wait!"

Arno bolted to his room. The projector was sitting on his shelf next to the toy robot that shot missiles from his head and light from his eyes. Arno knew that his robot took a 9-volt battery.

Arno slid the plastic cover off the back with shaky hands and removed the battery from inside. He tossed the emptied robot on his unmade bed and dashed to the kitchen to insert the battery into the back of the radio, fumbling in his hurry. He turned on the radio but accidentally knocked the front dial out of alignment so that all he got was static.

"Blast it!" he cursed.

He adjusted the dial and locked into his station just as the radio announcer was asking the last question.

"… is the ninth planet in our solar system, the farthest one away from the Sun, which makes Pluto the coldest planet we know. Pluto got its name from the Roman god of the underworld. The PL in the name also stands for the initials of Percival Lowell, the astronomer who caught hints of the planet twenty-five years earlier."

Arno knew all about Percival Lowell from one of Jean Slayter-Appleton's columns. An observatory named after him was now being used to create detailed maps of the Moon to prepare for a lunar landing.

Arno stood beside the telephone and dialed six out of the seven numbers for the radio station, which he had memorized. He stuck his finger in the hole of the last digit and got ready to dial it as soon as the announcer asked the last question, confident that he would know the answer. All he needed was to be the first to get through.

Meanwhile, his dad was laying slices of white bread on the only remaining clean counter to make ham sandwiches. Comet sat politely at his feet. He could smell the ham.

The radio announcer continued.

"First sighted in 1930, it turns out that Pluto is the smallest planet in our solar system. But

61

which, dear listener, is smaller? Pluto or our own moon?"

"Pluto!" Arno shouted as he dialed the last digit.

Arno pressed the receiver to his ear and held his breath.

His dad paused from spreading mustard on the sliced bread, but not on Arno's slices because Arno hated mustard.

Busy tone.

"Nooooo!" Arno slammed down the receiver and collapsed against the kitchen wall. Comet perked his ears in alarm.

"Maybe the caller will get the answer wrong," Arno's dad said.

"Any dipstick knows that Pluto is smaller," Arno said glumly.

"I didn't," Arno's dad admitted.

Arno stared at him for a long minute, then re-dialed the phone number except for the last digit. He stood with his finger in position on the dial while they both listened to the radio.

"Hello. You're our first caller."

"Hello!" the caller answered.

Arno's dad turned up the radio.

"Well, good luck to you because this is our

last question for the contest. Now, which do you think is smaller? Pluto or our moon?"

"Our moon, of course. Pluto is a planet."

"Wrong!" Arno whooped, and he dialed the last number.

"I'm so sorry," the announcer said. "That is incorrect. But thanks for calling. Who's next on the line?"

Arno couldn't believe his ears. The radio announcer's voice was speaking to him on the telephone!

Arno cleared his throat. He could hear his own nervous breathing on the radio. His dad turned down the volume so that Arno could concentrate.

"Arno. Arno Creelman," Arno stammered.

His dad gave him the thumbs-up sign.

"And how old are you, Arno?"

"Eleven, sir," Arno said.

"Eleven? My, my. With all this Space Race business going on, many kids tell me that they want to grow up to be astronauts, to be the first to land on the Moon. Is that your dream, too?"

"No, sir," Arno said.

"Oh?"

"I like telescopes. I want to discover new things that are way out there. Things that are so deep in space, it would take forever to reach them."

"What kinds of things?"

"I don't know. Maybe exoplanets."

"Exo what?"

"Exoplanets. Planets that might exist outside of our own solar system."

"Do you mean planets that orbit other stars?"

"Yes, sir."

"Other stars, not our sun?" the announcer asked.

"Yes, sir. I believe that many stars must have planets orbiting them. And once we discover them, there's a good chance some will have intelligent life. Maybe even more intelligence than here on Earth."

There was a long pause. It was as if the radio announcer didn't know what to say.

Finally, he spoke.

"That's certainly food for thought, Arno."

"I have plenty more ideas about outer space," Arno said. "I keep a list in my notebook, along with articles by Jean Slayter-Appleton."

"Wonderful! Speaking of which, how about we get back to the contest?"

"Yes, sir."

"Okay, then. If you've been listening, you'll know that our last caller got the answer wrong. Pluto is actually smaller than our moon."

64

"Yes, sir. I knew that."

"I'm sure you did. So, Arno, I'm going to ask you a related question."

Arno twisted the telephone cord around his hand and held his breath. What else was there to know about Pluto? He knew that Pluto moved on a different orbital plane than the other planets and that it actually crossed Neptune's orbit from time to time. He knew it took Pluto 247 Earth years to revolve around the Sun and over six Earth days to rotate. He knew it was the only new planet to be discovered so far in the twentieth century —

"Do you know how much smaller Pluto is than our moon?"

"Yes, sir! Pluto is only two-thirds the diameter of our moon."

Arno's dad's eyebrows shot up.

"And it's less than twenty percent of Earth's mass," Arno added for good measure, untwisting the telephone cord around his free hand.

Arno's dad's jaw dropped.

"Correct!" the radio announcer exclaimed. "You've just won the last invitation. We'll see you and your guest tomorrow night to help Jean Slayter-Appleton cut the ribbon. She's also promised to show visitors several of her favorite globular clusters from the new observatory's telescope. I'm not even sure what that is."

"A globular cluster is a dense collection of stars that form a spherical shape and are tightly bound by gravity," Arno said. "And when —"

"Wow," the radio announcer said. "Enjoy!"

"Yes, sir!" Arno shouted while Comet joined in the excitement by dancing a tight circle around him.

"Clear skies, Arno," the radio announcer said.

"Clear skies," Arno replied.

After he hung up, he beamed at his dad, who said, "Congratulations!"

"Thanks, Dad!"

Arno's dad cut the sandwiches into triangles and placed them on plates. Then he dropped some extra pieces of ham into Comet's bowl, which Comet devoured. "Who will you take as your guest?"

Meeting Jean Slayter-Appleton was serious business, and Arno didn't want anyone to spoil that. Especially anyone like Buddy.

"You, Dad," Arno said.

"I'd be honored," his dad said. He gave Arno a smile before placing the plates on the kitchen table. "What do you want to drink with the sandwiches?"

"I made lemonade this morning but it's all gone."

"Then ice water will do," his dad said. He opened the freezer. "Hey! What happened?" He held out the empty trays.

Arno explained about Buddy's astronaut endurance test.

"You should have heard him," Arno said. "What a scream."

"I'll bet," his dad said, filling the trays with water and putting them back into the freezer. He poured two glasses of milk instead.

"I also met the new kid on the block this morning. Robert."

"What's he like?"

"He's from London," Arno said. "Not England. Canada."

He didn't want to bore his dad by telling him about the astrology nonsense.

The telephone rang. Arno answered.

"Hi, Arno. It's Mindy."

Mindy was in the same grade as Buddy and Arno. She also lived on Arno's block. She had been Arno's science fair partner, and they made a tool that calculated what latitude they were from Earth's equator by measuring the angle of Polaris to the horizon. They came in second place.

Anton Spagnolli and Heimlich Fester won first place for their project about the revolutionary birth control pill and its predicted impact on society. Smaller families. Big deal. Both Arno and Mindy agreed they'd been robbed.

"Hi, Mindy. Guess what? I just won a contest to go to tomorrow night's opening of the new observatory."

"You did? That's fab."

"Thanks."

"Buddy told me you met the new boy."

"Yeah. Robert."

"My mom said she'll drive me to the movies this afternoon, and that I can invite him, you and Buddy."

"What's playing?"

"A new documentary about outer space!"

"Far out!" Arno buried the mouthpiece in his chest. "Dad, can I go to a movie about outer space? Please? Mindy's mom will drive."

"Sure." His dad dug out a dollar from his wallet and handed it to Arno. "So long as you make your bed right after lunch. You need to *earn* your allowance. Remember?"

"How'd you know I didn't make my bed?"

"Lucky guess." His dad pointed to the counters.

"And tidy all this while you're at it."

"Thanks, Dad!" Arno turned back to the telephone. "I can go," he said.

"Fab. We'll pick you up at one."

Grinning, Arno sat down to eat his sandwich. Winning a contest and now going to a movie about his favorite topic? What a great day!

After lunch, Arno's dad left the house to continue his rounds. He took Comet, who jumped up into the passenger seat and peered over the dashboard as if Shotgun was his middle name.

Arno stood in the driveway waving goodbye, the blazing Sun pounding on his head and shoulders, heat waves wafting up at his ankles. As the white van backed out, Arno got a clear view of the company logo.

Stinky's.

The boxy letters loomed large. There were lines of air wafting above the company name with a housefly weaving in and out as if overcome by the smell. Painted cartoon flames streaked from the wheel wells like a hot rod, only the flames weren't red or orange. They were painted baby-poop brown.

The whole thing was meant to be funny. And it had been until that fateful day Arno got trapped inside.

He shuddered to think about it, so he quickly went back inside. Besides, he had to make his bed and attend to the mess in the kitchen.

Every item in Arno's room had something to do with astronomy. The curtains had constellations printed on them. His bedside lamp was shaped like the crescent Moon. He had a large map of the solar system pinned to his ceiling above his bed. It featured data about each planet: its diameter, its distance from the Sun, its length of day and its axis tilt. On his bookshelf were his notebooks filled with "Clear Skies" newspaper clippings and his own deep thoughts.

He put his gutted robot back on the shelf beside the projector, then pulled up the sheets and smoothed out the bedspread, which was printed with spinning galaxies. He fluffed up his pillow and set it down just so. Done.

Arno paused to admire his clay solar system, the one he had built that morning, and forgot about the mess he'd made in the kitchen. He counted eight planets drying on his desk.

He frowned. Saturn was still under his bed.

Arno wished Comet was with him. Maybe he could coax the little dog to crawl under and retrieve the planet by making a game out of it. Comet was pretty gullible.

But Comet was bouncing around in the van with Arno's dad, looking forward to the ice cream cone that his dad would surely buy for him because he always did.

"Well, then, I'll just have to rescue Saturn myself," Arno said firmly, squaring his shoulders. "No sweat," he said. "Only take a second," he said.

Arno didn't budge. He didn't even bend down to try. He had made the mistake of picturing himself stuck under the bed, trapped, the weight of the mattress collapsing on top of him. His chest tightened, his breath became ragged, his mouth went dry.

Suddenly, Arno felt dizzy. He took a few staggered steps backwards until he stood in the door frame and leaned against it for support.

"Blast it," he said quietly.

The doorbell rang.

It was Mindy, putting him out of his misery.

FIVE

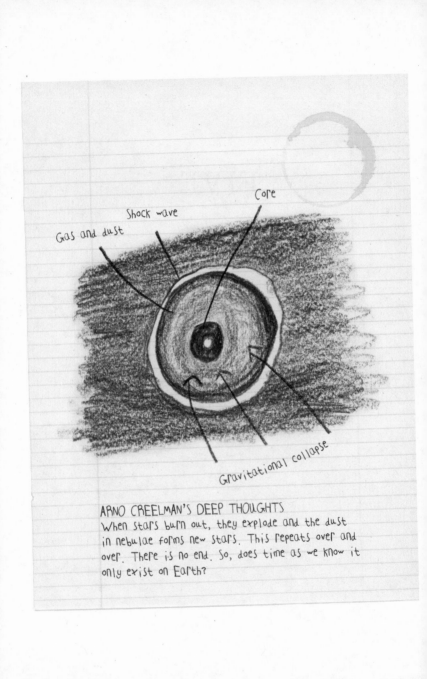

Gas and dust

Shock wave

Core

Gravitational collapse

ARNO CREELMAN'S DEEP THOUGHTS

When stars burn out, they explode and the dust in nebulae forms new stars. This repeats over and over. There is no end. So, does time as we know it only exist on Earth?

MINDY STOOD ON the front porch, her ponytail drooping against her neck in the heat, her long bangs twitching with each blink of her eyes. Mindy's mom sat in her sky-blue Ford Galaxie out front, with Buddy and Robert sitting in the back seat. All the car windows were rolled down.

Mindy was chewing gum but stopped as soon as Arno opened the door.

"What's wrong?" she asked with worry. "You look as if a giant asteroid is heading our way."

"Nothing. I'm fine."

Mindy's bangs twitched.

"Where's Comet?" she asked, looking past Arno into the house.

Mindy loved Comet. She rewarded him with dog biscuits whenever he rolled over for her, four paws flopping in the air. It had gotten so that as soon as Comet spotted her, he'd flip onto his back faster than the speed of light. She had a biscuit ready in her hand now.

"With my dad," Arno said. "Doing the rounds."

Mindy tucked the biscuit back in her pocket.

"Ready to split?" she asked, blowing the bangs out of her eyes.

"Yeah," Arno said, shutting the door behind him. "It's nice your mom's driving us."

"For you, maybe," Mindy said. "She's giving me the silent treatment."

"What for?"

"I kind of had an accident this morning."

"A *chemistry* accident?" Arno asked.

"Is there any other kind?" Mindy gave him a crooked smile.

Mindy owned the one and only chemistry set on the block. The set came with a real Bunsen burner, glass test tubes, beakers and flasks. It also contained a variety of dangerous substances that meant a lot of fun for any kid lucky enough to get to mix things with her.

Arno would never forget the day she unwrapped the set at her birthday party. The cover of the box promised it would introduce boys to the wonders of modern chemistry, and it showed a picture of a boy in a white shirt and tie who was pouring something from a test tube into a flask to create a mysterious puff of smoke.

Mindy flipped off the lid, blew the bangs out of her eyes and said, "Boys? *Boys?!* We'll see about that."

Later, she created such a cloud of stink, the sulfurous rotting-egg smell drifted all the way to Arno's house. That reek took weeks to get out of Mindy's curtains and bedspread, but only after repeated washings and being hung on the clothesline to dry.

After that, Mindy mostly followed the scientific method, but she was still not afraid to disregard instructions altogether and come up with her own experiments. She liked to tinker with chemicals and design her own concoctions. Potassium nitrate was one of her favorite ingredients. It was used in gunpowder, fireworks and rocket fuel. Sometimes, the results were explosive.

"The best inventions come from the unexpected," Mindy once told Arno while he studied the scorch marks running up the side of her garage door.

Arno followed Mindy down the porch steps and climbed into the back seat as Buddy and Robert scooched over to make room. Mindy jumped into the passenger seat next to her mom.

77

"Hello, Arno," Mindy's mom said, ignoring the pink bubble that Mindy began to blow with her gum. "Nice to see you."

"Thanks for inviting me," Arno said, barely remembering his manners as Mindy's bubble got bigger and bigger.

Mindy's mom adjusted her huge bug-eyed sunglasses, then pulled out and headed down the street. She was wearing a scarf to hide the curlers in her hair. Arno could tell that she was trying very hard to ignore Mindy, but when the bubble exceeded all laws of physics, she snapped.

"Cut that out!" she barked. "You're distracting me!"

Mindy popped the bubble and grinned.

"So, Robert," Mindy said, twisting around to face him in the back seat. "Tell us about yourself."

"Well, let's see," Robert said. "I'm from Canada, as you already know. My old man works for a big business machines company so we move a lot. That's a drag. My mom hates it here. She says no one speaks proper English."

"Oh, dear," Mindy's mom muttered.

"I like how you say 'mom,'" Mindy said. "Like it rhymes with 'gum.'"

He shrugged.

"I have a sister, but I wish I didn't," Robert continued. "She's in grade ten and she thinks she's Brigitte Bardot. She's a huge *American Bandstand* fan so she flipped out when that show was cut from ninety minutes to just an hour. But I'm glad. If I hear 'Venus' by Frankie Avalon one more time, I'll barf. What else? Oh! I was the star in last year's school drama. It was a gas."

Robert said "draa-ma," not "draw-ma."

"That's fab. Do you have a dog?" Mindy asked.

"No," Robert said, frowning. "Sorry. Just two cats."

"Do you like science?" Mindy asked.

"You bet I do," Robert said. "Especially astrology."

"Astrology isn't a science," Arno said.

"Sorry?" Robert said.

"You heard me," Arno said, leaning toward the open window to catch some wind on his face.

"Hey, Robert," Buddy said. "Do Mindy's astrology sign."

Arno gave Buddy a sharp elbow, which Buddy returned with the biggest toady smile ever.

"Okay, since you asked," Robert said. "Mindy. When were you born?"

"November 23rd."

"That makes you a Sagittarius. It means that you're happy, absent-minded, creative and adventurous."

"I'm not absent-minded," Mindy said.

"Is that so," her mom said, lowering her glasses to give Mindy a hard stare. "How about this morning, when you forgot to turn off your Bunsen burner? Quite the botch job."

Mindy blinked.

"Neat!" she said, turning back to Robert. "How'd you do that?"

"Astrology," Robert said, crossing his arms. "Which is a science."

"Bunch of hot air," Arno muttered.

"Sorry?" Robert asked again, leaning forward so he could see past Buddy to squarely face Arno.

"I said it's blowing hot air," Arno announced, which it was, with all the windows down.

He had just figured out that Robert was a lucky guesser who used general words that could describe lots of people. It was all a crock.

No one spoke for a few awkward minutes. Arno shifted his legs, which were sticking to the vinyl seat. He stared at the back of Mindy's neck. A few stray curls coming loose from her ponytail were sweat-soaked.

"Here we are," Mindy's mom chirped, pulling to the curb in front of the Capitol Movie Theater, which was designed to look like an old English stone castle.

Odyssey in Outer Space was printed in large blocky letters on the marquee.

Everyone spilled out onto the blinding sidewalk.

"I'll pick you up here right after the movie." Mindy's mom said. "Don't stray."

Everyone nodded, then headed inside, where the temperature dropped like an icebox.

"Air-conditioning," Robert said, grasping the fancy carved oak and brass railing. "Now *that's* Space Age progress. The Sun must be blasting 500 degrees today."

Robert said "progress" like "pro-gress," not "praw-gress."

"I love your accent!" Mindy said. "It's so fab."

Arno was not impressed. "Five hundred degrees?" he repeated. He wheeled around on the stairs to stop Robert in his tracks. "Is that what you think the Sun's temperature is?"

"More or less," Robert said with a shrug.

Arno scowled.

"Here we go," Buddy muttered to Mindy.

81

Mindy puffed her cheeks.

"Fun fact. The temperature at the surface of the Sun is 10,000 degrees Fahrenheit, 27,000 at its core," Arno said. "So, you're way, *way* off with your numbers."

"It's hot out." Robert rolled his eyes. "That's all I'm saying."

Arno studied him without blinking.

"I bet you don't even know what the Sun is made of."

"Of course I do."

"Okay. What?"

"Well, gas," Robert said. He paused to study the psychedelic pattern in the carpet. "I think."

"Can you be more specific?" Arno drilled, arms crossed.

"Arno," Mindy interrupted. "We should jet so that we can get dibs on good seats."

Arno stood his ground as waves of moviegoers bumped past. He took a deep breath because he was about to deliver one of his favorite speeches.

"Our sun is made out of hydrogen and helium atoms. It's held together by gravity and creates both light and heat in a process called nuclear fusion."

He took another breath and continued, while his audience shifted from one leg to another and looked everywhere but at Arno.

"Nuclear fusion rams atoms together, and our sun converts about four million tons of matter into energy every single second. It's a good thing Earth receives only a tiny fraction of the Sun's total energy or we'd be toast. The rest streams out into space."

Robert yawned. "Sorry," he said in his annoying accent. "Are you done?"

"It's the solar wind, or hot gas, coming from the Sun that blows past comets, giving them their long tails," Arno added. "As I mentioned before. Now I'm done."

"For now," Buddy added, loud enough for Arno to hear.

The four turned to march up the rest of the stairs and through the felt-covered doors into the semi-darkened theater.

It was already packed. Even the balcony was crammed. The few remaining empty seats were in the front row, and only two of them were together. Arno sat down at one end and Buddy quickly slid in beside him. Mindy and Robert moved farther down the row.

"Guess who I saw wearing cowboy boots in to-day's newspaper?" Buddy asked. "I'll give you a hint. My dad met him at NASA."

Arno wheeled on him.

"Listen up. I'm here to see a movie. So I don't want any more jibber-jabber from you."

"Get real," Buddy said. "I'd rather sit with Mindy and Robert any day but look around. Full house."

Arno did a quick scan.

"Blast it," he muttered as he settled into his leather seat and was forced to stare straight up at purple velvet curtains. The colossal marble statues at each side of the stage — women wearing robes and holding up torches — loomed overhead. Above him, the vaulted ceiling had been painted with clouds and stars.

"What a neck-breaker," Buddy complained. "Good thing I can tough it out like an astronaut."

Arno sighed.

He didn't want to be in a bad mood. After all, he was about to watch a movie about outer space! He listened to the happy chatter around him. He heard that the movie was a triumph of film art, that they would witness the solar system as it would look to a voyager rocketing through space.

They would travel into the farthest regions of the universe, past the Moon, the Sun and the Milky Way and into galaxies spotted by only the strongest telescopes!

Arno couldn't help but grin.

The curtains began to part, and the house lights dimmed to black. A hush swept through the theater.

At precisely that moment, Arno became acutely aware of the hundreds of warm bodies pressing forward from all the rows behind as well as the balcony above where smoking was allowed.

Arno caught a whiff of that smoke now.

What happens if there's a fire? he wondered. It was an odd thought, but he couldn't get rid of it. All that smoke! He glanced around for escape routes and only saw two exits way at the back.

That didn't look like enough for so many people.

His mouth went dry.

The movie opened with shot of a black star-filled sky, making the theater feel puny and cramped. Then the musical score exploded without warning. The audience flinched and covered their ears, Arno included. It was unlike anything he had ever heard.

There was relentless banging on the low notes of a piano.

Horns and trumpets blared when he least expected it.

Screeching violins stopped and started as the camera panned the cosmic scene and came across one massive celestial body after another.

It was disturbing.

Terrifying, even.

The jarring music, which seemed to be coming from every direction at once, bounced off the vaulted ceiling and came down on Arno's head. He felt as if the black theater walls were pressing in and the giant statues were in danger of toppling over, crushing everyone in the first row.

Arno gripped the armrests and squeezed his eyes shut, trying to catch his breath.

Please no, he thought. *Not now. Not in front of all these people.*

But it was happening. The dizziness, the tightness in his chest, the frantic thoughts of being trapped, of being smothered.

When he braved a look at the screen, a colossal asteroid was hurtling toward him, end over end, symphony horns bellowing.

It was deafening.

Arno jumped out of his seat and bolted up the aisle toward a dimly lit exit. He could no longer

86

hear the thunderous music because the sound of his pounding heart filled his ears.

Arno felt for the door and scrambled out into the lobby where he collapsed onto the first bench he came across. He sat with his head in his hands, gulping the popcorn-scented air.

"You okay?"

Arno looked up. An usher had followed him out.

"I ..." Arno shook his head, embarrassed. "Where are the restrooms?" he asked lamely.

"Down the hall to the left," the usher said, pointing with his flashlight.

He watched until Arno got up on shaky legs and turned the corner.

Inside the marble-tiled restroom, Arno stood at a sink and splashed his face with cool water. It helped, but he knew that there was no way he could go back inside the theater.

He dried himself and scowled at his pale face.

He couldn't call his dad to come get him. His dad was in the van doing his rounds with Comet.

Even if Arno walked home, what would he say to Mindy and the others? Her mom told them to meet on the sidewalk right after the movie. They would be worried if he didn't show up.

What if he told them the truth? That he had claustrophobia? Would they make fun of him?

Or worse, would they feel sorry for him?

Arno slipped into a quiet corner where he could still see the grand spiral staircase. His hiding spot was also out of sight from the concession counter where employees flicked popcorn at each other now that the lineups had disappeared.

Arno's mind raced. He thought he could manage his claustrophobia by avoiding triggers that brought it on. Only, his list of triggers kept getting longer and longer, expanding without end like the universe.

Being pinned down with a heavy wool blanket.

His dad's van filled with toppling baskets.

The Raleigh Deluxe Space Rider contest.

The narrow space beneath his bed.

Photos of cramped space capsules.

Dark, crowded movie theaters.

Calm down, he told himself. Sure, there were some things he could no longer do, things that weren't all that important in the great scheme of things.

But astronomy? He loved being in wide-open fields under giant nighttime skies with no danger of feeling trapped or crushed.

Arno held on to that thought with the gravitational force of twin stars orbiting each other.

When the theater doors finally flung open and people started to spill into the lobby, Arno got up from his hiding spot and mingled with the crowd.

"Hey!"

Arno turned. It was Buddy, who was rubbing the crick in his neck.

"What happened to you?" Buddy asked.

"The view from the balcony was better," Arno said. "Let's go find the others."

They made their way to the sidewalk where Mindy and Robert stood chatting in the raging sunshine.

"What a fab movie!" Mindy exclaimed as soon as she saw them.

Heads nodded all around, including Arno's.

Mindy's mom pulled up to the curb, and the four scrambled inside.

"That part about Mars maybe having vegetation?" Robert said from the back. "It blew my mind."

"Or that it would take four years moving at the speed of light to reach our next closest star," Mindy said.

"And what about Jupiter having twelve moons!" Buddy exclaimed. "Maybe I can visit one of them after I land on our own!"

"I learned a new word, Mom," Mindy said. "Nebula."

"What's a nebula?" her mom asked, adjusting her sunglasses.

"A nebula is dust that's left over from an exploding star. A super … super what, Arno?"

"A supernova," Arno said, realizing just how much he had missed.

"A supernova. It's a star that runs out of fuel and then explodes at five billion degrees!" Mindy added. She turned around to face Arno. "You're awfully quiet."

Arno shrugged.

"But you love outer space."

He shrugged again and looked out the window.

"Didn't you like the movie?" she pressed.

"Sure," Arno said. "But. You know. I already knew all that stuff."

"What about the ending?" Robert said. "I'm still thinking about that!"

"Me, too!" Mindy said. "I can't get my head around it. What do you think, Arno?" she asked.

What could he say?

"I can't get my head around it, either," he replied glumly, stuck in a car where it felt as if time was standing still.

SIX

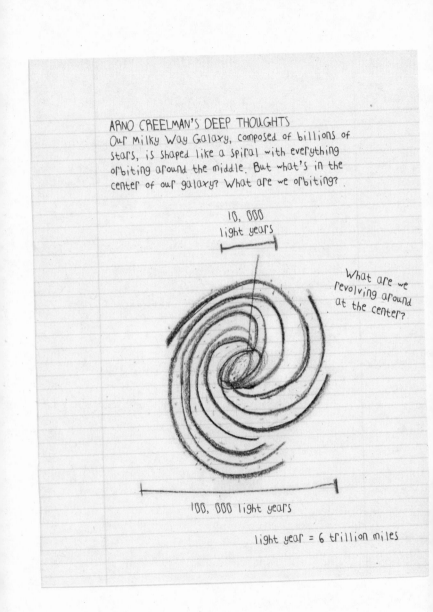

ARNO CREELMAN'S DEEP THOUGHTS
Our Milky Way Galaxy, composed of billions of
stars, is shaped like a spiral with everything
orbiting around the middle. But what's in the
center of our galaxy? What are we orbiting?

10,000
light years

What are we
revolving around
at the center?

100,000 light years

light year = 6 trillion miles

Everyone in the Ford Galaxie was quiet, each lost in their own deep thoughts.

"Can I turn on the radio?" Mindy asked her mom, breaking the silence.

Her mom nodded.

The radio station blared commercials for everything from cigarettes to television sets. Arno looked out his window while an ad played about the new Volkswagen Beetle, a little rounded car so different from all the other large tail-finned automobiles that surrounded them.

Then a Tang commercial came on.

"Did you know my dad's working on the Tang account, and he's trying to get astronauts to drink it once they get to outer space?" Buddy asked from the back seat.

"Yes!" Arno and Mindy replied in unison.

Mindy switched to another station, one playing a Motown song about a heat wave.

"Hey, Mom," Mindy said while bobbing her

head to the beat. "Arno won a radio contest this morning."

"You did?" Mindy's mom glanced at Arno in the rearview mirror. "What did you have to do?"

"Answer an astronomy question."

"He gets to go to tomorrow night's grand opening of the new observatory," Mindy boasted.

"I've been to an observatory," Robert said. "Back in Canada."

Arno leaned forward so that he could stare past Buddy to face Robert.

"You have?" he asked, genuinely interested.

"Sure. It was out of sight."

"What did you see?" Arno asked, all ears now.

"Jupiter. Saturn. I remember that. Oh, and a nebula just below Orion's Belt. That was really choice!"

Arno wanted to hear more. He wanted to hear everything!

"What about comets?"

"Sorry. I don't think so."

"What about galaxies?

"Galaxies?"

"You know, other than our own Milky Way?"

"I can't remember if we did. Sorry. It was a while ago."

"Oh, you'd remember a galaxy if you'd seen it!" Arno said. "They're huge!" Arno was excited. He couldn't help himself. "Fun fact. Our Milky Way Galaxy consists of billions of stars and adds about four new stars every year. But we now know there are countless other galaxies in the universe."

"So we've heard," Buddy said. "It was in the movie, remember?"

"Oh," Arno said. "Right." But he perked up again and added, "With the exception of a few of the closer galaxies, all of them are moving away from us so that the whole universe is spreading out with galaxies getting farther and farther apart!"

There was silence in the car.

Then Buddy said, "That was in the movie, too. You were there, weren't you? Up in the balcony?"

Arno clamped his mouth shut.

"Anyhow," Robert said, "we saw some neat things in the night sky, but what I'll never forget was the feeling of standing beneath that giant telescope. It was kind of scary."

"Scary?" Arno swallowed. "What do you mean?"

"Forty-five tons of steel and glass hung above my head, held in place by these enormous braces. I felt so small!"

"Hey," Buddy said. "That's how astronauts must feel climbing inside the space capsule of a massive rocket ship."

Arno remembered the photos of astronauts doing just that.

"Exactly," Robert said, confirming Arno's worst suspicion.

"What else do you remember about the observatory?" Mindy asked.

"Well, the roof was shaped like an upside-down bowl," Robert said.

He said "roof" like "rewf," not "ruhf."

"That's the dome," Mindy said. "Right, Arno?"

Arno barely nodded.

"Yes, the dome," Robert said. "It made sounds like thunder when it opened a slit to let the telescope peek through. We stood far below, waiting for our turn to climb this narrow staircase so that we could see into the eyepiece."

"Was it dark inside the observatory?" Arno asked. He couldn't help himself.

"Dark enough," Robert said.

"How many people were there?" Arno asked.

"I don't know. Maybe thirty. It was quite a small space so we had to crowd together. The giant telescope took up most of the —"

"How many exits were there?" Arno asked.

"How many exits?" Robert repeated. "Why?"

"How many?" Arno insisted.

"One, I guess. The same door we came through to climb up into the observatory."

Arno slumped back in his seat.

One exit. A crowd of people. A small space. Massive equipment pressing down. Dark.

Arno realized that he had never thought much about how it would feel to work in an observatory. If the observatory Robert had visited was in any way the same as the one that was opening tomorrow night, then Arno was sure to have a panic attack. Only this time, he'd have one right in front of his hero, Jean Slayter-Appleton.

And that would dash any hopes he had about becoming an astronomer.

Each of these thoughts hit him in rapid fire, like a meteor shower.

"What's wrong?" Mindy asked. "You look like you've discovered a DSO."

"A what?" Arno asked numbly.

"DSO. Deep Sky Object." Mindy paused. "Like in the movie …"

Buddy wheeled on Arno. "You must have fallen asleep up there in the balcony."

Arno's face burned.

"Get a grip! Arno wouldn't fall asleep during a movie about outer space!" Mindy said.

"I didn't fall asleep," Arno said gruffly. "It was just a dorky movie."

Mindy gasped with surprised hurt. Buddy shifted uncomfortably in his seat. Robert gave an awkward cough.

"Here we are," Mindy's mom announced, pulling to the curb in front of Arno's house. "Have fun at the opening of the observatory," she said.

None of the others said a word.

Arno walked up his driveway without looking back, but he could feel everyone staring at him with the searing heat of an exploding supernova.

He crossed his front porch and went inside. No family. No Comet. It felt as lonely as the far side of the Moon. He stood for a minute, trying to decide what to do.

He could go back to his room and look through his astronomy book to find a new activity. There was an interesting one about building a star clock out of two disks that could be dialed and lined up with the North Star, Cassiopeia and the Big Dipper to tell the time at night.

Arno slumped. Why bother? He'd never become a real astronomer.

It was the saddest thought he had ever had. He felt tears coming on, standing there alone in his house.

Arno walked into the kitchen and picked up the telephone. He dialed the number his mom had posted on the refrigerator in bright orange crayon.

"Hi, Aunt Faye," he said. "It's Arno."

"Hi, Arno," she said. There was a crisp edge to her voice.

Arno could hear a baby wailing in the background.

"How's the new baby?" he asked politely.

"Hungry," she said. "Like always. Is everything okay?"

"Yes," Arno said with a choke while twisting the telephone cord around his free hand.

Silence, except for the baby.

"Did you want to speak to your mom?"

"Sure," Arno said.

Arno listened to voices and the howling baby, who wasn't even stopping for air. Then he heard his mom on the telephone.

"Hello, Sunshine!"

"Hi, Mom."

The sound of her voice and his nickname made him want to pull up a chair to sit down. He did.

"What have you been up to?" she asked.

Arno thought he'd start with something funny.

"I watched Buddy stick his feet in a bucket of ice water."

"Another astronaut endurance test?"

"Yeah," Arno said. "You should have heard him screech. It was hilarious."

"I'll bet. What else is new with you?"

"I made a solar system out of clay. It accurately shows the relative sizes of each planet."

But then Arno remembered Saturn, and that made him sad all over again. He wilted a bit in his chair.

"Sounds wonderful. I can't wait to see it," she said.

Arno didn't want to talk anymore about the solar system with Saturn under his bed, impossible to recover.

"I met the new kid down the street. Robert."

"What's he like?" she asked.

"He thinks astrology is a science."

"Is that so," she said. She sounded amused.

Arno regretted bringing up Robert. Robert had spoiled Arno's excitement about the observatory.

"I won a radio contest for tickets to the new observatory," he said.

"Congratulations!"

"Thanks." Arno paused. "I'm not sure I want to go."

"What? You love astronomy! That's all you ever talk about. And you'll get to meet your hero … what's her name? Jill Something-Apple Pie?"

Arno chuckled. He knew his mom was kidding.

He remembered the night in the backyard after he'd given a slide presentation of the eighty-eight constellations to his family using his Show Me projector in the living room.

He had promised a stellar show, but his brothers sat glumly on each end of the couch, arms crossed, sucking the life out of the room like twin dark stars. Even Arno couldn't ignore the snoring after only thirty minutes in.

When he turned on the lights, there was a smattering of polite applause, with both brothers and his dad rubbing their eyes and stretching as if they had woken up from a nap.

Upset, Arno fled to the backyard, collapsed into one of the lawn chairs and lay face up to take in the beauty of the universe.

He heard the back door squeak open. His mom came outside. She spotted Arno, then grabbed another lawn chair to sit beside him. She looked up.

Nobody spoke for several minutes.

"Oh, look. A shooting star," she said, pointing.

"You know it's not really a star, right?" Arno said. "It's just dust that heats up and glows when it hits Earth's atmosphere."

He knew he was being crabby, but he didn't care.

"I know," his mom said. "Let's see if I can find the Big Dipper."

"You don't need to do this, Mom," Arno said, still staring straight up.

"Don't be silly. I want to find it and then the North Star, like you told us in your talk."

Arno softened. She had actually listened to him.

She studied the night sky.

"There it is," she exclaimed, pointing again. "Now, where's the North Star? You said to draw a line between the two stars at the front of the ladle and follow that to the next bright star. Oh! There it is!"

"Polaris. The North Star that all other stars appear to circle around," Arno said. Then he added, "Good job."

They quietly lay there.

"There's a double star in the handle of the Big Dipper," Arno said. "Triple if you look through a telescope. I forgot to mention that."

"Really?"

His mom studied the handle. She squinted.

"I can't see it."

"I can. It's the second star from the end. It was used as an eye test for entering the army in ancient Athens and Sparta."

"I must be getting old." His mom sighed. "My eyes aren't as good as they used to be. I guess I need a telescope."

They lay there some more. It was a clear night. The sky was breathtaking.

"Thanks, Mom," Arno said.

"For what?"

"For listening."

"Oh, Arno! I loved your talk," she said. She gave his hand a squeeze before going back inside.

The next day, she came home with a telescope called a Moonscope, with its tripod included. He knew it cost a whopping amount — $19.99! —

105

but his mom explained that everyone in the family, even his brothers, had agreed to chip in.

That night they pointed it at the Big Dipper.

"Well, look at that," his mom said, staring through the eyepiece. "There really is a double star in the handle. And I can see the third one, too. Amazing."

And it was.

Arno rocked back in his chair. The mess he had made emptying the kitchen drawers was still on the counters, and Buddy's scuff marks still marred the floor.

"Come on, Mom! Jill Something-Apple Pie?" Arno repeated on the telephone. "Her name is Jean Slayter-Appleton." He twisted the phone cord in his hand. "I know she'll be there. But …"

Should he tell his mom? Should he admit he had claustrophobia? Would it make any difference? It wouldn't take away the fear, he knew that.

And that's what he so desperately wanted. But now he realized his mom couldn't do that.

"But what?" she pressed gently.

Arno was doing everything he could not to cry. The baby was still wailing and Arno could hear his aunt calling out to his mom, something about a rash.

"What's wrong, Arno?" his mom said, ignoring Arno's aunt and the bawling baby.

Arno swallowed.

"Nothing," he managed. "It's just that I'm worried there won't be clear skies tomorrow night. That's all."

"Oh," she said, sounding relieved. "Of course. You can't have a cloudy night blocking the telescope's view of the universe. Well, I'll keep my fingers crossed for you."

"Okay. Thanks, Mom."

The baby's wailing got louder.

"I'd better run. Clear skies, Arno," his mom said.

"Clear skies, Mom," Arno said back.

He hung up and wished for clouds.

SEVEN

KILLER
ASTEROID

Dust from impact would block the sun

Moving at 44,000
miles per second

ARNO CREELMAN'S DEEP THOUGHTS
What are the chances that life on Earth
will be destroyed by an incoming asteroid
of a large comet?

ARNO WAS SURPRISED to hear his dad at the front door, along with Comet's antsy pitter-patter on the tiles. It wasn't even close to dinnertime.

"Hey, Dad," Arno said. "You're early."

Comet made a beeline for his water bowl.

"It's too hot for Comet in the van," his dad said. "I'm dropping him off, but I'll be home in an hour or so."

Comet emptied his water bowl and scampered up to Arno. Arno got on his knees to play-wrestle. He flipped Comet onto his back and paddled his paws in the air.

"Say uncle," he teased.

Squirming, Comet wagged his tail in glee.

"How was the movie?" his dad asked.

Arno stiffened.

"Everyone loved it," he said, straightening up.

Arno's dad headed back out but added, "No more treats for Comet until dinner. He just polished off his own ice cream cone. Then he knocked mine out of my hand and wolfed that, too. I think it was deliberate, the rascal."

Arno poured himself a glass of ice water and filled Comet's bowl. He took both out to the porch, then dropped into one of the chairs and flipped through his stack of *Life* magazines while Comet slurped some water, then sprawled beside him.

Arno settled on the issue with a chimpanzee in a spacesuit on its cover. The astrochimp was named Ham, and he had been specially trained for space travel, the first primate launched in a rocket as part of America's space program. Arno opened up to the article, which he had read several times already.

Beginning in July 1959, the three-year-old chimpanzee was trained to do simple, timed tasks in response to electric lights and sounds. Then, on January 31, 1961, Ham was secured for Project Mercury and was launched from Cape Canaveral, Florida, on a suborbital flight that lasted just over fifteen minutes. The whole time, he had his vital signs and tasks monitored using computers back home.

Ham's lever-pushing performance was only a fraction of a second slower than on Earth, and this proved that tasks could be performed in space.

His capsule splashed down in the Atlantic Ocean and was recovered by a rescue ship later that day. He only suffered a bruised nose.

Too hot to read any further, Arno lay back in his chair. He was about to close his eyes, when he spied Buddy wheeling toward him on the street, his cowboy boots pumping like a rodeo clown. He carried a large box under one arm and steered with the other so that he wobbled along the way. He pulled up onto Arno's sidewalk and leaned his bike against the porch steps. He marched up to where Arno sat and collapsed into the empty chair beside him.

Comet lifted his head, blinked at Buddy, then flattened back down.

Arno turned a page of his magazine and methodically scanned the photos, hoping Buddy would see that he was otherwise engaged.

Buddy eyed Arno's glass of ice water.

"Got any Tang?" he asked.

Arno shot him a glare. Buddy's toad smile was all the more annoying.

"Just kidding," Buddy said. "Look what I have." He held up the box and shook it. Jigsaw pieces shifted inside.

"A puzzle?" Arno said. "So what?"

"Not just any puzzle. A *modified* puzzle. This is another astronaut test," he explained, as if Arno couldn't have guessed.

Arno said nothing. He didn't want to play along, although a small part of him knew that he'd enjoy watching Buddy put himself through the wringer once again.

He didn't have to wait long. Buddy was unstoppable when he was on a mission. He flipped off the lid. The box was filled with puzzle pieces. Buddy had written numbers on the plain backside of each piece.

Arno plucked a puzzle piece from the box. It had the number "56" written on its back. Still, he said nothing and dropped it back into the box, knowing that his lack of enthusiasm would be small torture to Buddy.

Buddy burst into explanation.

"So what you do is, you put the pieces together by placing the numbers in the right order, row after row."

"Sounds too easy. How is this an astronaut test, exactly?"

Buddy smiled his toady smile. He reached into his back pocket and pulled out a pair of leather gardening gloves, adult-sized.

"You have to do it wearing these," Buddy said.

"That's ridiculous," Arno said.

"Is not! With practice, this test will improve hand-eye coordination. And that's critical in a space capsule with control panels. Ask any astronaut."

"I'll bet," Arno said drily. He held up the *Life* magazine photo spread of Ham at the controls. "It's not like any *monkey* could do it."

Buddy's face darkened.

"Hey! That monkey had *years* of training."

Arno tossed the magazine on top of his stack. Reading was impossible with Buddy around.

"Here," Buddy said, waving the pair of gloves in Arno's face. "You give it a try."

"I'd rather watch," Arno said. "Wow me."

Buddy emptied the box onto the deck. He flipped all the puzzle pieces over so that the backs with the numbers faced up.

"No cheating," Arno said, pointing to the gloves.

Buddy sat back on his haunches and pulled on the gloves. Then he bent over the pieces.

He didn't get very far and he didn't get very fast. He fumbled and muttered and fumbled some more. He tried sandwiching a piece between two gloved thumbs to fit it into another piece. He tried licking the pointer finger of a glove and pressing down on a piece to see if it would stick long enough for him to rotate it. He tried wedging one piece under another, then sliding the top piece off into position.

Nothing worked well or consistently.

Buddy's face turned redder and redder. Beads of sweat covered his forehead and upper lip. The back of his T-shirt grew wet.

Comet got up like an old man, lazily sniffed a few puzzle pieces, then flopped down on his other side, his back to the whole scene.

Meanwhile, Arno leaned over to assess Buddy's progress while taking sips of his refreshing ice water.

"Should I be timing you?" he asked.

"Very funny," Buddy said.

It had been fifteen minutes, and Buddy had not even fitted two pieces together.

"Good thing we're not in a real emergency situation," Arno said, noisily crunching down on an ice cube. "Like if an asteroid was hurtling toward Earth, and your job was to blast it out of the way with the push of a button."

"Arrrrrgh!" Buddy exclaimed. He sat back on his heels, then peeled off his sweaty gloves. "It's just too hot."

Arno burst out laughing.

116

But the heat was getting to him, too.

"I'll go get us some Popsicles."

Comet looked up.

"And some more water for Comet."

Comet thumped his tail.

Arno struggled out of the chair, his energy zapped by the heat. He picked up Comet's empty water bowl and went inside. He ran the tepid water in the faucet for a while, hoping it would run cooler. It was a losing battle.

A losing battle, Arno realized, just like visiting the observatory tomorrow night without having a panic attack. He sighed. He let the water run through his fingertips as he sank into his sad thoughts.

Then he heard barking.

Comet's bark.

An excited bark.

Arno filled Comet's bowl, then rushed outside.

He couldn't believe it! Comet was sitting in Robert's rear bicycle basket, and Robert was wheeling him up and down the street in a figure-eight pattern. Buddy and Mindy were clapping on the sidelines, cheering Comet on.

Comet wagged his tail in delight, as if Circus Act was his middle name.

117

"Hey, back off!" Arno shouted at Robert.

Robert slowed down and put his feet on the hot pavement for a full stop. All eyes turned to Arno, including Comet's.

Arno stormed over, water sloshing out of the bowl he was carrying.

"You have no right!" Arno yelled, planting himself in front of Robert's handlebars. "Comet's my dog!"

"I wasn't hurting him." Robert sounded genuinely hurt. He reached around to scratch Comet behind the ears.

Comet licked Robert's hand. It was too much!

Arno tossed the bowl to the ground and plucked his little dog from the basket. He set Comet on the dry grass in front of the bowl, which was now mostly empty. Comet hung his head.

"I said no!"

Arno was shaking with fury, and it didn't help that everyone was still staring at him in surprise.

Mindy blew the bangs out of her eyes.

"We're sorry, Arno," she said. "We didn't mean to scare you. Comet came down the porch steps when he saw me and Robert, and we were just keeping him company until you came out."

118

Her words floated toward Arno like the Milky Way softening the night sky. Arno turned from being furious to being embarrassed. He knew he was being a jerk, but then again, his plan to become an astronomer lay in ruins.

All he could do was make grumpy noises as he scooped up Comet and the water bowl and marched back to his front porch with as much dignity as he could muster.

Comet scooted underneath Arno's chair, his tail wedged between his legs, and Arno set the now-empty bowl beside him. His dog made a pitiful whimper. Just one, but it was enough to crush Arno completely. Arno dumped the few ice cubes remaining in his glass into Comet's bowl. The little dog wagged his tail and happily crunched the ice cubes from beneath Arno's chair.

All was forgiven.

As Arno slouched in his chair, Mindy, Robert and Buddy whispered in a huddle on the street. Arno knew they were talking about him, the way they kept glancing his way. Then the three edged toward Arno's front porch, Robert leading the trio.

Arno's shame melted as quickly as the ice cubes Comet was crunching. His anger flared.

"Hey, there, Arno. Mind if we join you?" Robert called out hesitantly as they approached the steps.

"I'm reading," Arno barked.

He scowled as he grabbed a random issue from his stack and opened it to a dog-eared article, one that he had read plenty of times.

It was about the planets.

When Robert reached the top step, he cautiously leaned forward to have a look.

"Cool! The planets! One of my favorite topics," he said brightly.

"I doubt it," Arno said. "This is about science. *Sci-ence*. Not fortune telling."

"Hey," Mindy chimed in. "It's too hot out here to bicker. I'm sure Robert wants to hear about planets just as much as the rest of us."

"Not me," Buddy said. "Planets are for babies compared to space flight."

All three stared at him.

"Think about it," he continued. "Rockets. Heat shields. Flying through zero gravity. Astronomy's boring in comparison."

It was all Arno could do not to go ape. Yes, Robert had completely ruined Arno's career, but was he truly to blame? After all, he didn't know about Arno's claustrophobia when he talked about the observatory. And yes, Mindy should have sided with Arno, but then again, all she really wanted was for everyone to get along.

But, *Buddy*?

Buddy knew full well how much astronomy meant to Arno. And now he threw it in Arno's face like a vicious knockout punch by Floyd Patterson in the twelfth round.

It was too much.

"Boring? You think astronomy is *boring*?" Arno demanded with such force, Comet jumped to all fours.

"Boring. That's right. I said it. *Bor-ing*. Boring with a capital B."

"Unbelievable," Arno said, his face on fire. "If you think you'll be flying around in outer space one day without a basic understanding of astronomy, then you better think again."

"I know enough," Buddy said, crossing his arms.

"Is that so," Arno said. "Let's just see."

He returned to his article about planets and flipped to a page that showed a full-color drawing of each of them arranged in a grid, three by three.

"Pop quiz," Arno announced as he turned the magazine around so that Buddy could see it. Arno randomly pointed to one of the drawings. "Which planet is this?"

When Buddy didn't immediately respond, Arno added, "I'll give you a hint. It's the smallest one in our solar system."

"Pluto," Buddy blurted. "And I don't need any hints."

"Easy guess," Arno said. "What about this one?"

He pointed to another planet. It was yellowish.

"I know!" Mindy jumped in. "It's named after the Goddess of Love."

"Venus," Buddy said after a pause.

"Don't help him," Arno said, eyes narrowing. "And this?" He pointed to an orangey-brown one.

"Jupiter?" Buddy said it like a question.

"Are you asking me?" Arno asked, eyebrows raised.

"Jupiter," Buddy said nervously.

Mindy and Robert applauded.

"According to astrologists, Jupiter is linked to good luck and bounty," Robert said.

"Get real," Arno said. He turned back to Buddy. "What about this one?"

He pointed to a dark gray planet.

"Is that our moon? Buddy asked.

"Is our moon a planet?" Arno asked.

"No." Buddy paused. "Then that must be Mercury."

"You're running out of planets," Robert said in a sing-song way. "And Buddy's passing with flying colors."

Arno scanned what was left. Buddy absolutely deserved to fail because he had insulted astronomy. But all that remained of the solar system was Saturn with its giveaway rings, Earth with its all-too-obvious blue oceans and white clouds, blueish Neptune, blue-green Uranus, and red Mars. Everyone knew Mars, Arno reasoned, so he had to decide between Neptune and Uranus.

Buddy interrupted his thoughts.

"Hey. You said the Moon wasn't a planet."

"It's not," Arno said. "It's Earth's only natural satellite."

"Then why is the Moon on this page?"

"What you mean?"

"Well, this one here is Mercury, right?" Buddy pointed to Mercury, which was dark gray and not the Moon.

Arno nodded.

"So *this* one must be the Moon." He pointed to Mars. "You're trying to trick me."

"What are you talking about?" Arno asked. "That's Mars."

"It can't be Mars," Buddy said. "Look at it. It's almost exactly like Mercury."

Robert and Mindy leaned in with Arno to have a better look. It was nothing like Mercury. It was red. It was Mars, all right.

"Busted!" Robert said. "You got all the tricky ones, but you messed up on the red planet."

Buddy looked at Robert, then Mindy.

"He's right," Mindy said with a shrug. "Mars is easy. You can't botch that one."

"Fun fact," Arno added. "Mars is red because the iron in its rocks rusted over time. Mars used to have more liquid water and an atmosphere that contained more oxygen, which caused the rusting that we see today."

Buddy stared at the picture of Mars. He blinked.

Then, without another word, he left the porch, got on his bike and pedaled away.

"Something we said?" Robert asked.

"Weird," Mindy agreed.

Arno tossed his magazine back on the pile. He looked at Buddy's abandoned puzzle on the deck. Another failed astronaut test. But this time, it didn't feel good kicking Buddy when he was down.

Comet hung his stubby tail as he watched Buddy disappear.

EIGHT

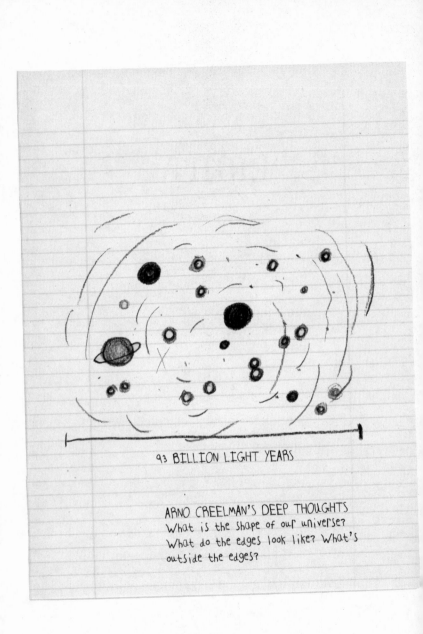

93 BILLION LIGHT YEARS

ARNO CREELMAN'S DEEP THOUGHTS
What is the shape of our universe?
What do the edges look like? What's
outside the edges?

Right after Buddy's unexplained departure, Mindy and Robert bailed, too.

"I should cut out," Mindy said to Arno. "I left an experiment cooling in my garage."

"I'll come with you," Robert said, and they headed for her house.

Abandoned on the porch, Arno and Comet dozed in the heat. When Arno woke up, the Sun was starting to draw longer shadows from the trees that lined his street. It was almost dinnertime.

As he got up to go inside, he noticed that the lid of the mailbox beside his front door was ajar. Arno's heart did a little skip when he saw that the latest *Life* magazine was among the bills and letters. All new articles to read!

Arno dropped the mail onto the front hall table, then scanned the contents of the magazine.

He gasped. There was an article about Pluto! Arno wanted to dig right in.

But wait! Maybe he could use his excitement in an experiment. Arno rooted through the drawer of

129

the hallway table and found a flashlight. He tested the batteries with the on/off switch. Perfect!

He took the magazine and the flashlight to the front hall closet. He opened the door and, taking a deep, steadying breath, squeezed inside and sat down beneath the jackets hanging above his head.

"You coming?" he asked Comet, who had been traipsing after him the whole time.

Comet lowered his little head slightly, but obediently followed Arno into the closet. Together they sat facing each other. Arno closed the closet door.

It was dark. And smelly. There were a lot of his brothers' giant sneakers heaped beneath the jackets.

Arno reasoned that if he could somehow focus on his excitement about astronomy, then that would keep his mind off triggers that caused a panic attack. No panic attack, no claustrophobia. And if he practiced here in his front hall closet, then maybe he could pull it off at the observatory.

It was worth a shot.

Arno turned on his flashlight and flipped to the new article about Pluto, a tiny planet so far away that no space probes had ever reached it. Arno read that when Earth and Pluto were on opposite sides of the Sun, there was so much space, it was

130

hard to understand. To better appreciate the distance, the article suggested that the reader make a paper model.

Perfect, thought Arno. If he read the instructions about how to make one, he would picture the steps in his head. That would keep his mind off other things, like how dark it was inside, how cramped he was sitting there, all those coats hanging over his head like —

Arno shook it off.

The article said to cut a piece of adding-machine paper that was as long your outstretched arms could reach. Then it said to write "Sun" on one end of the paper and "Pluto" on the other end. Arno could easily imagine completing that step.

Got it, he thought.

Next, he was instructed to fold the paper in half. *At the crease, mark "Uranus."*

Got it, he thought. He felt great.

Fold the paper in half again, dividing the strip into quarters. Mark "Neptune" on the crease nearest Pluto. Mark "Saturn" on the other crease.

Still following, he thought, picturing where the planets were landing on the creased paper.

Fold the Sun up to Saturn and make a crease. Mark that crease "Jupiter." Fold the Sun up to Jupiter

131

and make a crease. That's where the orbit of the asteroid belt is located.

Neat, thought Arno. He knew all about the asteroid belt.

The asteroid belt was occupied by numerous potato-shaped bodies called asteroids that circled the Sun. "Asteroid" meant starlike, and these rocks were too disrupted by giant Jupiter's gravity to have ever formed a planet. Arno also knew that the total mass of all the asteroids equaled four percent of Earth's moon.

Arno braved a small smile at Comet. His head was filled with exciting astronomy facts, just as he had planned. He wasn't thinking about the dark, tight space he was reading in at all.

Except, as soon as he realized *this* thought, he felt a slight but familiar flutter in his stomach. Ignoring it, he quickly returned to his article to keep his mind busy with intriguing astronomy information.

Fold the Sun up to the asteroid belt and make a crease. Mark this crease "Mars."

Got it, Arno thought. Still, he couldn't help notice that his mouth had gone dry. He tried to swallow.

Fold the Sun up to Mars but leave it folded. Fold the crease side up to Mars again.

Oh, no, Arno thought. The air inside the closet had become stuffy and suffocating. He tried to read on, but the words on the page got wobbly.

This will leave you with three new creases between the Sun and Mars: one for Mercury, Venus and Earth.

Arno was no longer following. He could no longer think. He tried to chase the bits and pieces of instructions, but it was like trying to catch all the stars coming out during a new moon on a clear night.

He felt dizzy. His heart started pounding hard against his ribs and he couldn't breathe. The dark, tight space where he sat cross-legged pressed heavily against him. He grabbed the door handle and fumbled out of the closet, his flashlight and magazine spilling out onto the floor.

Red-faced and humiliated, he lay gulping air. Comet scampered out and licked his face.

Arno slowly picked himself up.

His experiment was a complete failure.

A complete and utter failure.

And now he knew for sure. He *had* to get out of going to tomorrow night's opening of the observatory.

But how?

He heard his dad's footsteps on the front porch, coming home for the day.

Comet scrambled to the door greet him.

"What's wrong?" Arno's dad asked as soon as he stepped inside and spotted Arno on the floor.

"Just horsing around with Comet," Arno said, getting up.

"What's with the flashlight?" his dad asked, spying it beside the open closet door.

Arno thought quickly.

"I was checking the batteries. I might do some astro-drawing tonight," he said.

Pinned to the bulletin board in his bedroom were several of his charcoal-and-pencil drawings of the night sky as seen through his telescope. He was getting really good at drawing under dim conditions, with his flashlight covered in red film so as not to disturb his night vision.

His dad nodded, then fished into his pocket to pull out his wallet.

"We're having your mom's tuna noodle casserole for dinner," he said, handing Arno fifty cents. "A tall cold glass of lemonade would be perfect to go with it. Can you run over and pick up a bag of lemons at Tasty Fresh?"

Arno nodded, grateful for the distraction.

—

Arno lingered at Tasty Fresh Foods longer than he needed to while carting a bag of fresh lemons, just to enjoy the cooler air inside. He strolled up and down the aisles but stopped in his tracks when he turned the corner and came across the brand-new display of Sweet Cheeks disposable diapers.

Sweet Cheeks took up almost half the aisle.

Arno stood gobsmacked.

Disposable diapers? What were they? He scanned the promises on the packages.

Comfortable.

More absorbent.

No more washing.

No more washing? What? Once they got dirty, you just threw them out? That didn't make any sense.

But its claim to use space-age technology to construct the disposable diapers offended Arno the most.

"Blast it," he said under his breath.

Still. Would families really go for these new-fangled no-cloth things, throwing them out after only one use?

Arno knew how many diapers a baby was expected to dirty before being fully toilet trained. It

135

was a fun fact that his dad often told customers, to startling effect.

Six thousand!

When they learned that staggering number, they gratefully hired his dad's service.

Arno set down his bag of lemons. He pulled a package of Sweet Cheeks diapers off the shelf for closer examination. The package featured a toothless smiling baby, one who was particularly adorable with its pudgy legs and naked chest, the words *Sweet Cheeks* arching in jolly letters above its round, bald head.

Arno pictured his dad's company name on his fleet of white vans.

Stinky's.

The name was no longer funny. He didn't think his dad would be laughing, either.

Arno set the package back on the shelf. He slowly stooped to pick up his lemons and slunk to the nearest checkout. He felt like a traitor for even considering that Sweet Cheeks might put his dad's diaper-cleaning service out of business.

Back at home in the kitchen, which Arno's dad had tidied without too much scolding, Arno cut up the lemons and did his best to avoid squirts to the eyes.

"Hey, Dad. Tasty Fresh is selling disposable diapers."

His dad was pulling the casserole out of the oven. He stood to face Arno while holding the bubbling hot dish with oven mitts.

"I know," he said.

"I didn't think there was such a thing. Sounds kind of crazy to me."

"Well, it's the Space Age after all. People want things that are modern and easy."

"Are you worried?" Arno asked.

"About disposable diapers eating into my business? There might be some impact," his dad admitted. "But my customers are loyal. They want the best for their babies. And I've been in this business a long time."

"You and your father before you," Arno chimed in.

It was Arno's grandfather who had started the family business. Arno's dad smiled.

"Don't get me wrong. I'm all for new discoveries. Take the Space Race. I think we should constantly look outward, beyond our horizons, to advance. And something interesting always happens when we do."

"Like what?"

"Like no matter how far we travel, we always turn around to look back at where we've been. When we do, our perspective changes forever."

"I guess," Arno said, not really following.

But then he thought about all the times he had spent looking through his telescope. He was constantly on the hunt for something new — a comet or a double star, depending on the season. But after every session, he'd return to one of his favorites: the Andromeda Galaxy, the Orion Nebula, the Beehive Cluster.

"Like astronomy," Arno said. "I keep a list of what I've seen but I always go back to the ones I already know. And it reminds me. The more I know, the more I don't know. I realize I'm nowhere close to the edges of the universe."

"Precisely. When we finally get to see what Earth looks like from the Moon, I imagine that our perspective will change forever. Only then will we understand just how small and fragile our planet is, and that we each need to do our part to protect it."

Arno had never heard his dad talk to him like this. Such deep thoughts! It was wonderful.

While his dad slipped the hot casserole onto the stove and took off the tinfoil, Arno opened the dish cupboard. He set two places on the table, then turned to study his dad.

His dad had changed out of his uniform, but his Stinky's van was proudly parked in the driveway, a van he drove day after day after day. It was as unglamorous a job as Arno could imagine, picking up dirty diapers from neighbors, then washing and replacing them with soft folded cotton that smelled sweet, like sunshine.

Arno didn't want to spoil the mood, and he didn't want to be mean about it, but still. He had to ask.

"Dad, what's your part?"

Arno's dad was rooting through a drawer for a serving spoon.

"Disposable diapers may be easier," he said, "but I guarantee that they'll cost more money in the end, and they'll certainly create way more garbage. More garbage can't be good for the Earth. I think my service will stand the test of time."

Arno nodded. He pictured Stinky's van. He liked those bold boxy letters. He liked the dizzy fly and the poop-tone flames. It *was* still funny!

"How come you never talk to any of us about joining Stinky's once we grow up?" Arno asked.

"I'd be happy if that's what one of my sons wanted. But mostly I hope that each of you make

139

your own way doing whatever it is you love to do. Like astronomy."

Arno frowned.

"Maybe. Maybe not," Arno said. "I could help you instead."

It was a desperate offer. Arno knew it even before he said those words out loud.

"Arno! Nobody I know understands more about astronomy than you. You're going to do great things, make huge discoveries that I can't even imagine." Arno's dad paused. "Is everything okay?"

Arno swallowed the lump in his throat.

"Yeah. Why?" he managed.

"I phoned your mom today. She said you called her."

"Yeah, to say hi."

"She said you sounded … troubled."

Arno turned away to stare out the window. He wanted to tell his dad, he really did. The words were there at the tip of his tongue. What was stopping him?

If he admitted his fear of small, dark spaces, would his dad be disappointed? If he admitted his fear of being crushed by surrounding walls, would his dad be embarrassed for him? If he admitted his fear of suffocating, would his dad tell him that everything would be okay, even though they both knew it wouldn't?

His fear was real and there was nothing anybody could do for Arno.

"I miss Mom. That's all."

"She said you mentioned that you were worried about the weather. That there might not be clear skies for tomorrow night."

"Well, there's no point going if it's cloudy."

"No. I don't suppose."

Arno peered outside once again. All he could see was a blindingly blue sky.

NINE

ARNO CREELMAN'S DEEP THOUGHTS

If objects move away from us at the speed of light, then these objects would be forever invisible to us. But could their light reach us by coming around the universe from the other direction?

Earth has a surface area but no edge

Universe has a volume but no edge

AFTER THE DINNER dishes were washed, Arno's dad asked if he still planned on doing some astro-drawing.

"Looks like clear skies," his dad said, peering out the kitchen window at Venus, the evening star making its early appearance.

Arno didn't have anything better to do, and besides, it was a great way to practice his observation skills and forget about his troubles.

He gathered the things he would need.

His Moonscope was propped on its tripod by the back door. His astronomy notebook was in a drawer of his desk, along with his pencils and smudging tools. His pocket star atlas was in the same drawer. He had left the flashlight on the table by the front hall closet. He wrapped red cellophane over the end of it. That was held in place with an elastic band.

Then he took everything outside and dragged a lawn chair to the middle of the backyard. He set up the telescope and pointed it to the Moon.

145

Arno sat back and waited for it to get darker. Venus was now very bright, and there was Mars with its red hue. One by one the stars came out, the brightest summer ones making a beautiful triangle. Vega. Altair. Deneb.

As the sky grew its darkest, he could see the galaxy. He could even make out its dust lanes when looking straight up, the dark cloudy areas with even more densely packed stars behind them, their light blending together like spilled milk.

Arno adjusted his telescope and scanned the Moon's terminator — the line between the lit part and the shadowed part. He stopped when he spotted an interesting X shape made from the ridges of a cluster of craters that were still lit by the Sun.

It was so striking, he decided to sketch the scene.

He got out his B pencil and drew a circle in his notebook. Within that, he started to outline the peaks, the borders and the internal walls of the craters. He drew in the shadows with a softer, darker 8B pencil and erased where the sunlight hit the tops of the craters to bring out the whitest of whites.

The X shape was starting to pop off the page and then —

"Whatcha doing?" a voice called out from Arno's back door.

It was Buddy. He swept his bright, unfiltered flashlight beam across the yard and locked in on Arno.

"Turn that thing off!" Arno barked while covering his eyes. "You're ruining my night vision!"

"Oops." Buddy fumbled with his flashlight to turn it off, then dragged another lawn chair over to where Arno was positioned.

"Are you *drawing*?" Buddy asked.

Obviously, Arno was drawing. He had a pencil in his hand and his notebook on his lap!

"In *this* light?" Buddy asked.

Obviously, he *was* drawing in the dim red light he had created with his covered flashlight to protect his night vision.

"Why?" Buddy asked.

"I'm practicing my observation skills."

"Can I see?"

Arno sighed. He moved away from the eyepiece to make room for Buddy, but in his haste, Buddy knocked the telescope so that it was now pointing somewhere else in the universe.

"Whoa!" Buddy said, looking through the eye-piece. "I never knew there were so many stars. You can't draw that!"

Arno nudged him aside to see what Buddy was looking at. It was the constellation Hercules, near the bright star Vega.

"Yes, I can," Arno said. "I use something called triangulation. I draw the locations of the brightest stars that I spot within my eyepiece, then use their locations to see where I should add the next brightest stars. Then I use those to draw the next brightest ones until I work my way down to the dimmest ones, the ones I can barely see. I have to use averted vision for those last ones."

"What's averted vision?"

"It's where you don't look directly at something because it disappears if you do. You can only see it if you look slightly away. It works for things in the night sky that are very faint."

"So, you have to have good eyesight to be an astronomer," Buddy said.

"Yeah," Arno said, looking at his sketch. "Of course."

"Like an astronaut," Buddy said.

"I guess."

Arno paused. He stared at Buddy.

Buddy stared back. He gulped. It looked as if he was fighting back tears.

"What?" Arno asked.

"I can't see the color red," Buddy said so softly, Arno could barely make out his words.

"You can't see red?" Arno repeated. "Like on apples or Stop signs?"

Buddy sat down, his head in his hands, staring glumly at the grass that was black between his feet.

"So that's why you didn't recognize Mars," Arno said.

Buddy did not even look up.

"You're color blind."

Buddy gave a small nod.

Arno realized that Buddy was having trouble speaking. But why? Color blindness wasn't so bad, was it?

Then he understood the awful truth. Astronauts could not be color blind. They would need perfect vision for all those instrument panels in their space capsules. Any confusion about which button to push, which warning light to read, which lever to pull could mean explosive disaster.

"And you didn't know until today?" Arno asked.

Buddy glanced at Arno. He wiped at his eyes.

Arno had no words for Buddy. Buddy's career as an astronaut was over just as surely as Arno's astronomy career.

There they sat, the telescope between them, silently staring up at the glorious heavens where both their dreams exploded like supernovas.

A lonely dog barked in the distance, bringing Arno back to Earth.

"Oh, look. There's Jupiter," Arno said, always glad to spot that familiar friend.

"Where?" Buddy asked half-heartedly.

Arno pointed to it. "The bright one that's not twinkling. Planets don't twinkle."

"I knew that. Only stars twinkle."

"Stars don't really twinkle either," Arno said. "It's just that they're so far away, they look like pinpoints of light. And because all that light is coming from a single point, when it goes through our thick, wavy atmosphere it looks as if the star twinkles. But planets are much closer. They look like tiny discs, not pinpoints of light. So our atmosphere doesn't get in the way as much."

Arno repositioned his telescope. "If Jupiter had been eight times bigger, it would have used its hydrogen to explode and become another burning star. But it stayed a planet. Right now I can see all four of its largest moons. One of them is as big as Mercury."

"Really? Let me see!" Buddy said.

Arno moved aside.

"I can't find Jupiter," Buddy said, bumping the telescope again, then aiming it all over the northern hemisphere.

"Move away," Arno said. He repositioned the telescope once more. "Now look again, this time with your hands behind your back. Don't *touch* anything."

Buddy did as he was told.

"I see it!" he exclaimed. "And I can see pinpricks of light in a line beside Jupiter. Are those moons?"

"Yes," Arno said, happy that Buddy was interested for once. "Galileo was the first to see them with a telescope back in 1610. He proved that not everything orbits around Earth, which was what everyone thought. That's why the telescope is the most important invention of all time."

"Far out," Buddy said.

"Galileo also discovered that our moon isn't smooth. It has mountains and craters. And that the Milky Way wasn't just a smear of light but is made up of billions of individual stars densely packed together. And that the Sun has sunspots."

"It'd be cool to see sunspots."

"Don't ever look directly at the Sun, Buddy."

Buddy moved away from the telescope.

"I'm color blind, Arno. I'm not an idiot."

"Right. Neither was Galileo. He made more discoveries that changed the world than anyone has ever made before or since."

"And now we have the Space Race," Buddy said gloomily.

Arno solemnly nodded.

"And now we have the Space Race."

They wallowed in the silence that followed, knowing that they wouldn't be a part of it.

Still.

It was hard to ignore the glory right before their eyes.

"Want to see the biggest object in the night sky?" Arno asked.

"Why not," Buddy said.

"Okay. See the constellation that looks like a big W on its side up there, opposite the Big Dipper?" he said, pointing.

Buddy followed with his gaze.

"That's called Cassiopeia. The right side of the W makes a deeper V and it can be used as an arrow that points in the direction of the Andromeda Galaxy. Now hold your arm straight out."

Buddy did.

"Move a fist and a half below that arrow. See the galaxy? Like a small pale puff of smoke?"

"That faint fuzzy thing?" Buddy exclaimed.

Arno repositioned the telescope.

"Hands behind your back. Have a look."

Buddy peered into the eyepiece. His jaw dropped.

"Look near the center of that galaxy," Arno instructed. "See how it's brighter? That's where there are the most stars. Now use averted vision to look at the outer regions that are less bright. It gives you a good idea about its size."

Buddy stared at the galaxy.

"It's spiral-shaped like our own Milky Way Galaxy," Arno continued. "And it's spinning, just like ours."

"How far away is it?" Buddy asked, still hogging the eyepiece.

"About two and a half million light years," Arno said. "So, it takes two and a half million years for light from that galaxy to reach our eyes. You know what that means?"

"What?"

"You're now looking two and a half million years back in time. When that light started out, Earth was entering into the last ice age. Some stars you see right now probably no longer exist."

"How does that even work? Buddy asked.

"It's like an echo of someone shouting. Even though they're not shouting anymore, you can still hear the sound of their voice."

Buddy slowly pulled away from the telescope but continued to stare up at the universe.

"I never thought of astronomers as time travelers. You're lucky. Tomorrow night in the observatory, you'll see stars even farther away."

Buddy's words caught Arno off guard. He looked down at his unfinished sketch.

"I'm not going," he said quietly.

Buddy whipped his head around to face Arno.

"Have you lost your marbles? Astronomy is all you ever talk about."

"I have claustrophobia."

"Claustro … what?"

"A fear of being trapped in small spaces."

"That's a thing?" Buddy asked.

"That's a thing," Arno said.

"Okay. But what does that have to do with the observatory?" Buddy asked.

"I'd worry that the giant telescope might crush me or that the dome might collapse or that people would crowd the exit and I'd be trapped and couldn't breathe. I'd panic."

"But those things won't happen," Buddy said.

"It doesn't matter. The fear's real," Arno said. "So, I can't go."

Buddy thought for a minute.

"Astronauts have fear," he said.

"Come on, Buddy. Get real."

"No, listen. They do. My dad told me that many things can go wrong inside a rocket ship, and the astronauts know that. But they still complete their missions. Know how?"

"No. How?" Arno asked.

"They learn tricks about how to get the job done even though they're afraid."

"Yeah? Like what?"

"Like focusing on something that's not threatening. Like breathing slowly and deeply and counting to three on each breath. Like picturing something happy, maybe their home or their kids. And they tell themselves over and over that the bad thing they're afraid of is not going to happen. That way, they don't bolt. They stay put and keep working until the panic passes."

Arno blinked.

Maybe he'd been on to something with his experiment in the front hall closet. Maybe he quit too soon.

The boys stared up at the night sky.

"Oh, look," Buddy said. "A shooting star."

Arno was about to say, "You know it's not a star, right?"

But he stopped himself.

Instead, both boys said nothing for a long time. The Earth continued to orbit the Sun. But when Arno stared up, slowly tracing the universe's constellations with his eyes, he thought he caught a glimmer of hope.

The weather broke in the middle of the night, cracking the air in half.

Arno woke to a loud clap of thunder, followed by lightning that filled his bedroom with a jagged flash. He sat up on his elbows in bed, enjoying the cooler air that rushed in through his open window. The curtains billowed. He looked at the time on his sun-shaped alarm clock.

It was 2:15 in the morning.

Another clap of thunder roared so deeply across his neighborhood, Arno could feel it in his chest.

Then came the first sounds of rain spattering against the roof, waves of tiny pings.

Arno turned on his lamp. The instruction booklet he had long memorized for his Moon-scope lay dog-eared on his night table.

Oh, no!

He had left his telescope outside!

What would happen if it got soaked in the rain? Arno did not want to find out.

Blast it!

He kicked off the covers and hit the cold floor with his bare feet. He didn't stop for slippers. He bolted from his room and headed to the back door as fast as the speed of light. The rain was starting to come down hard.

Arno tramped across the spongy grass to where two lawn chairs were still positioned in the middle of the yard for nighttime viewing of the heavens. The telescope stood dripping on its tripod be-tween the chairs.

Arno scooped up the works and turned back just as Comet streaked past him. Comet, who slept on his bed in the kitchen at night, must have followed Arno out the door.

"Here, Comet!" Arno called while patting his thigh, a hand signal that Comet knew well.

Another bolt of lightning blinded the sky, followed by a round of thunder even deeper than before. Arno knew it was dangerous to be standing out in the open. He could be struck at any second.

Comet yelped. Wild-eyed, he tore around and around the yard, as if he was looking for an escape hole in the wood fence. He seemed too scared to see Arno, let alone listen to him.

Arno was getting soaked. Rain streamed down his neck. His pajamas stuck to his shoulders, back and thighs. His telescope wasn't getting much protection tucked under his arm.

"Comet! Comet!" he called, but it was no use.

Terrified, Comet kept orbiting Arno in wide circles, yelping and yelping and paying no attention to anything other than his own cosmic-sized fear.

Arno didn't know what to do. Comet was bolting way too fast to catch.

Then Comet spotted his doghouse, a home-made shed with a pitched roof and painted siding that matched Arno's own house.

Comet scampered inside.

Arno did not want to leave him there. His little dog was clearly terrified, and the storm had only just begun.

He needed to rescue Comet. But how?

TEN

ARNO CREELMAN'S DEEP THOUGHTS

Space is silent because there is no air to carry sound waves. But what would space sound like if we could change electromagnetic particles moving through it to something our ears could hear?

Sun = 99% of all matter in our solar system

THE RAIN TEEMED down. Still hugging his telescope under one arm, Arno crouched in front of the doghouse door, which wasn't a door at all. It was a small archway cut into the front of Comet's house.

Arno peered inside. He couldn't see a thing. Comet must be huddled at the very back where it was as dark as shadows on Pluto.

"It's okay, Comet," Arno called out in a soothing tone.

Comet whimpered.

Another clap of thunder shook the ground.

There was more whimpering from the back of the doghouse. And then Comet howled. It was the most pathetic sound that Arno had ever heard. He couldn't leave his little dog there. He couldn't! But Arno was soaked now, and he was starting to shake from the cold night air.

"Come here, Comet," Arno pleaded through the door. "Let's go back inside. It's safer there. And you can sleep in my bed. You can even have the pillow!"

Comet still didn't budge. Why would he, what with the horror that was going on outside?

Arno thought some more.

"Do you want a cookie?" he coaxed. "Come, Comet, and I'll give you a nice cookie."

Nothing.

"Two cookies."

Nothing.

Then Comet made new sounds, forlorn sounds, as if he was weeping.

Arno gulped. He would have to keep Comet company until the storm was over. But now he was shivering uncontrollably. He had no choice but to climb inside the doghouse where it was drier, where he could scoop up Comet and hold him until he could calm down.

Arno stuck his head through the door. His stomach tightened. What he saw was his worst nightmare.

The inside of the doghouse was an unbearably cramped space and as black as a cave. But it was an unbearably cramped space that smelled of a sopping wet, terrified little dog.

Arno thought back to his conversation with

Buddy, the one about how astronauts must finish their missions even when they were afraid.

What were the tricks they used?

Arno could barely think because of the deluge of rain, a white noise that sounded like what he imagined space would sound like if it could be heard. Also, his shivering and the rising panic from the pit of his stomach made him feel as if he might throw up, pass out, or both. He was breathing hard, gulping at the damp, heavy air. He desperately wanted to bolt back inside his house, into his safe, cozy bed.

"Astronauts don't bolt," he said out loud. "They stay put and keep working. They remind themselves that the panic will pass."

Arno glanced around the yard once more, still bucketing with rain. He steadied himself.

"I'm coming in," he announced to Comet, straining to keep his voice calm.

Arno decided to back in on his hands and knees. Slowly, he inched his way inside — first his bare feet, then his legs, his hips, his back and his chest. It was a tight squeeze when it came to his shoulders, but he pushed on. He ducked his head through the door and pulled in his telescope.

He sat up.

He was inside.

Comet leaped into Arno's lap. His little body was shaking with terror, but he licked Arno's cheek all the same.

Focus on things that are not threatening.

"Good dog," Arno said to Comet as he always did whenever Comet gave him a kiss.

Then Arno heard his own labored breathing.

Breathe slowly and deeply and count between breaths.

Arno forced himself to slow down, to suck in air until his lungs were completely full and then slowly let it out. He repeated this again and again, counting between breaths until he had a nice steady rhythm.

Picture something that makes you happy.

Arno could see a sliver of the backyard from the doghouse door, where the lawn chairs sat under the night sky. He remembered the time with his mom when she discovered Polaris, the North Star, and then bought him his most prized possession.

That thought made him feel warmer.

Tell yourself that the bad thing will not happen.

Arno studied the cramped space surrounding him. He was getting his night vision so he could now make out the walls and the roof that was merely inches above his head. He reached out and touched the sturdy walls. He touched the solid roof. He could feel that nothing was about to collapse.

When Arno came to the end of Buddy's advice, he went back to the top of the list and repeated his thoughts.

Comet is with me.

Breathe in. One, two, three. Breathe out. One, two, three.

My telescope is out of the rain.

The walls are sturdy. The roof is solid.

How many times he chanted this string of thoughts, he could not say, but when he eventually paused, he noticed that his heart was not pounding as hard.

"It's okay," Arno said to Comet on his lap. "I've got you."

And then he repeated his chant. Again. Again. And again.

The rain poured down, drumming off the roof above their heads and forming puddles all around. But inside, Arno and Comet were in good company. When Arno paused from his chanting once more, he could feel that his heart was beating normally, that his breathing was soft and easy, that his mouth was no longer dry.

His panic had slipped away.

After that, Arno just sat, stroking Comet's head.

Time passed. At some point, Arno heard his name. It was his dad calling from the back door. A flashlight beam was frantically sweeping the yard. Arno popped his head out of the doghouse.

"I'm in here!" he called back.

The rain was slowing down. Arno also noticed that all the lights in the house were on. His dad must have been madly searching for Arno in every room.

Arno's dad ran across the yard and crouched in front of the doghouse. Water was dripping off his face.

"What are you doing in there?" he asked.

"Rescuing Comet," Arno said. "He got scared in the storm and wouldn't come out. I didn't want to leave him alone."

"See if you can hand him to me," his dad suggested, holding out his arms.

Arno scooped Comet from his lap and shoved the squirming dog through the archway.

"Come on inside," his dad said, and he turned back to the house, sheltering Comet against his chest.

Arno grabbed his telescope, crawled out and made a dash for the back door.

Everyone stood dripping in the kitchen.

"I'll go get us some towels," his dad said.

He set down Comet, who trotted over to nudge his food dish now that the danger had passed.

Arno gave him a cookie, then a second one like he had promised.

Once they dried off, Arno's dad offered to make hot chocolate. Comet curled up in his bed in the kitchen, and Arno covered him with his blanket.

"You really gave me a scare," his dad said, heating the milk. "How did Comet get outside, anyway?"

"I remembered that my telescope was in the backyard when it started to rain. When I went out to get it, Comet made a dash."

"Does the telescope still work?" his dad asked.

Arno dried it with a tea towel, then peered through the eyepiece out the window at a distant light. He used the dials to focus.

"Yup," Arno said with relief. He set the telescope in the corner near Comet's bed. Comet lay there, his eyes shut tight, his chest slowly rising and falling.

"Don't worry about the weather," Arno's dad said. "These dramatic summer storms come in the night but they always pass quickly. You'll see. You'll have clear skies for the observatory."

The observatory! Arno was about to make excuses, but he caught himself.

Didn't he just work through a panic attack in the doghouse? Didn't his chanting do the trick? If he could do that once, maybe he could do it again. The fear might always be there, but even so.

He had rescued Comet. Now maybe he could rescue himself.

He would go to the opening. He would brave that mission.

He *would* become an astronomer.

"It's going to be great," Arno said.

And he meant it.

Arno sat at the kitchen table where his dad placed two steaming mugs. Arno wrapped his cold hands around one of them.

"Your mom called this evening after you went to bed," his dad said. "She said the baby is falling into a nice little routine so she's coming home Sunday. She said to tell you that she counted all the ways she misses you and it's more than eighty-eight constellations."

Arno smiled. "That's astronomical." He took a warm sip. Delicious.

"We also talked about inviting the new boy's

family for dinner," his dad continued. "Buddy's family, too. For a barbecue."

Robert and Buddy over for hot dogs. It wasn't the worst idea.

"Time for bed," his dad announced when they finished their hot chocolate.

It had stopped raining. Only the gutters dripped.

They headed upstairs, turning the lights off as they went. When they got to Arno's room, his dad spotted Arno's clay solar system still drying on his desk. He went over to admire the planets, surprised by how small Pluto was compared to the rest of them.

"Fun fact. Of all the mass in the solar system that is not our sun, more than half is in Jupiter," Arno said, holding up that giant planet as proof.

"Wait now," Arno's dad said. "There are only eight planets here. Where's Saturn?"

Arno knew precisely where Saturn was. His stomach immediately did its fluttering thing, but that only reminded Arno he could use the practice.

"I'll get it," he said.

And his dad watched curiously as Arno knelt to peer under his bed.

More Fun Facts

So much has happened since Arno's first visit to an observatory.

Tang, the instant breakfast drink, began to be used by astronauts in 1962 when it was added to the menu for John Glenn, the first American astronaut put into orbit aboard *Friendship 7* (the Mercury program). During that and subsequent flights, NASA was able to learn how eating was affected in low gravity. Tang sales certainly improved after astronauts started drinking it. This association created the misconception that Tang was invented *for* the space program.

After twenty-seven-year-old cosmonaut Yuri Gagarin made his historic flight into space aboard *Vostok 1* on April 12, 1961, the Soviet Union launched the first woman into space on June 16, 1963. Valentina Tereshkova completed forty-eight orbits around Earth during almost three days in space. She was twenty-six years old.

Recognizing that space exploration should be done only for peaceful purposes, the United Nations created a *Treaty on Principles Governing the Activities of States in the Exploration and Use of Outer Space, including the Moon and Other Celestial Bodies*. The treaty was signed by the United States, the Soviet Union and the United Kingdom on January 27, 1967, the same disastrous day that the Americans lost three astronauts (Roger Chaffee, Gus Grissom and Ed White) to a fire in their spacecraft during a launch rehearsal test as part of the Apollo program.

On December 24, 1968, a famous photograph called "Earthrise" was taken during the *Apollo 8* mission by Bill Anders, one of the first astronauts to orbit the Moon. The photo is of Earth and parts of the Moon's surface. It is widely recognized as the most influential environmental photograph ever taken.

The Space Race dramatically ended on July 20, 1969, with the landing of *Apollo 11* on the Moon after just over three days of travel from Earth. Michael Collins continued to orbit the Moon while Neil Armstrong and Buzz Aldrin landed on the surface in the lunar module called *Eagle*, then walked about and conducted experiments for around three hours.

Before returning to orbit to join Collins, the two astronauts stuck a US flag on the Moon and also left a plaque that read:

HERE MEN FROM THE PLANET EARTH
FIRST SET FOOT UPON THE MOON
JULY 1969 A.D.
WE CAME IN PEACE FOR ALL MANKIND

On July 24, 1969, all three astronauts came back to Earth safely.

Twelve astronauts in all walked on the Moon from 1969 to 1972. Their footprints remain.

For more than a decade, tensions remained high between the two superpowers. Both sides were also critical of each other's engineering. The Soviet spacecraft was designed with automation in mind to minimize risk due to human error by having fewer manual controls for cosmonauts to manage. The Americans designed their complicated spacecraft to be operated by highly trained astronauts. Then, in July 1975, the Apollo-Soyuz Test Project was conducted. This was the first *joint* US-Soviet space flight. It involved the docking of the Soviet *Soyuz 19* spacecraft with an unnumbered Apollo vehicle that was surplus from the terminated Apollo program. It provided useful engineering experience for future joint US-Russian space flights as well as the International Space Station.

In 1976, two NASA probes arrived at Mars. Photographs were taken of the planet, and its rocks were analyzed. However, the search for life was unsuccessful.

In 1981, *Columbia*, the first of NASA's reusable space shuttles, took its maiden flight. The shuttle made space travel routine and eventually opened the path for a new International Space Station.

In 1986, the returning Halley's Comet was met by a fleet of five probes from Russia, Japan and Europe. The most ambitious was the European Space Agency's *Giotto* spacecraft, which flew through the comet's coma and photographed the nucleus.

In 1990, the Hubble Space Telescope, the first large optical telescope in orbit, was launched using the Space Shuttle. Unfortunately, it was crippled by a problem with its mirror. A complex repair mission in 1993 allowed the telescope to start producing spectacular images of distant stars, nebulae and galaxies.

In 2006, the definition of a planet changed. According to new rules adopted by the International Astronomical Union, a celestial body must meet the following three criteria in order to qualify as a planet: a planet must be round, a planet must revolve around the Sun, and a planet must have "cleared the neighborhood" of its orbit. This means that as a planet travels, its gravity sweeps and clears the space around it of other objects. Some of the objects may crash into the planet, others may become moons. Pluto only meets the first two criteria. It has not cleared its neighborhood.

Pluto is now considered a dwarf planet. It joins Ceres (located in the asteroid belt between Mars and Jupiter) and Eris as our solar system's dwarf planets, along with Haumea (discovered in 2004) and Makemake (discovered in 2005). Both are located between Pluto and Eris.

Back in the 1960s, *Life* magazine resorted to artist drawings of what Pluto might look like because there weren't any photographs of it yet. The first spacecraft to visit Pluto and take photographs was NASA's piano-sized *New Horizons*, launched on January 19, 2006. That craft benefited from a gravity assist from Jupiter and made its closest approach to Pluto on July 14, 2015.

In the early days, the first astronauts had to undergo extreme physical and mental screening to ensure that they would respond effectively and appropriately to stresses associated with space missions. Physical endurance tests included treadmills, tilt tables, keeping one's feet in ice water and blowing up balloons until exhaustion. There was also lengthy time spent in sensory-deprivation chambers. And, like jet pilots, astronauts had to see all colors. Later, during the Space Shuttle era, NASA created a new astronaut job assignment called Mission Specialist. This attracted people from many different fields, such as doctors and teachers. For these positions, NASA relaxed some physical requirements. For example, astronaut Roger K. Crouch is a payload specialist, an expert who has trained to conduct experiments for single space flights. He is color blind.

With the aid of more powerful devices, additional moons were discovered around Jupiter. Today's total now stands at well over seventy, making Jupiter the planet with the highest number of moons in our solar system. Astronomers believe that, because of its strong gravitational pull, Jupiter has saved Earth from many impacts from cosmic debris.

As scientists continue to strive to understand our universe, the countdown has just begun. Astronomers use ever more powerful telescopes and other devices to search for objects that might strike Earth. They use them to predict solar flares that could knock out our power grids. They use them to search for exoplanets and perhaps even to discover alien life.

All the while, NASA is once again forecasting crewed missions, only this time the plans are for returning to the Moon to establish a permanent outpost, landing on an asteroid and orbiting Mars, all by 2035.

Perhaps you'll be on one of these missions!

Or perhaps you'll make an unimaginable discovery in deep space through even more sophisticated telescopes than we have today.

Clear skies!

Acknowledgments

I was encouraged to write this novel by the late Sheila Barry, who edited seven of my previous books. She told me that Arno Creelman was one of her favorite characters in *The Spotted Dog Last Seen* and *The Missing Dog Is Spotted*. In both of those novels, he's an old man who used to work in a planetarium and had an extensive astronomy library. Together, we wondered what Arno might have been like as a young boy.

Sheila never got the opportunity to read the manuscript. I was too late.

My mom, Mary Ronaldson, helped me with the 1960s cultural references. During a recent visit, she told me that when she was growing up on a farm on the prairies in Alberta, it felt as if she could practically reach out and pluck the stars from the sky. Now when she looks up, she can no longer see them because of her failing vision. It

179

makes me appreciate the beauty of the night sky all the more.

I'd like to thank the readers who kindly shared their feedback on early versions. My husband, Peter Kerrin, read the first version for me and provided much encouragement, as always. He is my Polaris, my very own North Star who unfailingly provides guidance whenever I'm feeling lost. Incidentally, he built his own telescope from scratch when he was a boy.

Early readers also include Charles Follini and his class at Fountain Academy of the Sacred Heart (Halifax, Nova Scotia) and Michele MacKinnon and her class at H. M. MacDonald Elementary School (Antigonish, Nova Scotia).

Although this is a work of fiction, I attempted to include accurate scientific references. For that, I thank John A. Read, telescope operator at the Burke-Gaffney Observatory in Halifax, Nova Scotia, and author of several astronomy-related books, as well as Patrick Kelly, lecturer and editor of *Observer's Handbook*, Royal Astronomical Society of Canada (2007–11). Both read versions of this manuscript and provided their valuable advice. If there are errors, I would have inadvertently introduced them in the final version. My apologies to astronomers and astronauts everywhere.

I also greatly benefited from taking Douglas (Tony) Schellinck's course called "Guide to Observing the Night Sky with Binoculars," which included some winter star parties in the environs surrounding Halifax, and from attending meetings of the Royal Astronomy Society of Canada (Halifax Centre) where Tony and other members shared their wealth of expertise and jaw-dropping photography. That was me in the back row.

I am most grateful to Shelley Tanaka, who stepped in to help shape and edit this work. She served as editor on a number of novels I admired by other authors, and so I was very pleased to benefit from her expertise. Her constellation of editing notes, comments and penciled-in smiley faces were stellar. I would like to thank Michael Solomon for the design of this book, Emma Sakamoto for her notebook interpretations of Arno's Deep Thoughts, and Katy Dockrill for her cover illustration.

I've seen photographs of astronauts who wore cowboy boots. This includes Chris Hadfield, the first Canadian astronaut to walk in space, as well as American Gene Cernan, the last astronaut to walk on the Moon during that pioneering era. I don't know if John Glenn ever wore cowboy boots, but he was a childhood hero to me and he was kind enough to sign *Martin Bridge: Ready for Takeoff!* — my first-ever published children's book, which featured a boy with a rocket on its cover.

Arno's astronomy hero, Jean Slayter-Appleton, was inspired by Helen Sawyer Hogg (1905–1993). She was a Canadian astronomer and the first female president of several astronomical organizations, having conducted pioneering research into variable stars (stars with fluctuating brightness) and globular star clusters (sphere-shaped formations of stars and the oldest parts of our galaxy) in a time when many universities would not award scientific degrees to women. Hogg found creative ways to continue her career, such as bringing her baby daughter to the observatory at night while she worked. She was also known for her popular weekly column "With the Stars," which was published in the *Toronto Star*. She believed the stars belong to everyone and authored a book by that name.

I only vaguely remember the landing of *Apollo 11* because I was quite young at that time. However, I grew up with *Star Trek* and then *Star Wars* and all the space movies that followed. I confess I was inspired by Captain Kirk and the idea of space travel. And, like Buddy, I thought *I* might become an astronaut until I was forced to wear glasses way back in grade two.

Still, I hope to one day witness a crew landing on Mars, for surely the first Moon landing and the first Mars landing would serve well as my life's astronomical bookends.